Valley of Dragons Book 1:

The Guardians of the Valley.

Fanny Garstang

As the biggest fantasy fan between us this one is for my husband even though he still hasn't read it. But he did help me work out the direction it needed to go in.

One

Lulizen ran through the gardens of her mountaintop home with courtiers looking on in confusion. Ferns covered the rockery garden that ran either side of a processional way across the enclosed garden, hiding the stone path she ran along. On two sides were small cloisters of rooms. At the top of the garden were her parents' rooms around the throne room and opposite was a gatehouse leading to a cobbled yard where all visitors to the walled palace were made to wait in a waiting room on one side of the gatehouse.

Following the short young woman, the best they could were three servants; her two maids and one of her father's advisors. She shouted, "I'm not, I'm not."
She stumbled in her unsuitable silk slippers and the plants caught at her trailing skirts. She was dressed for an audience with an important visitor though they wouldn't see her. From servant gossip she had heard her father was planning a marriage with this important guest and that was what she was running from. A maid cried out, "Luli, please."

"All you father wants is for you to see." The advisor called out as he struggled behind with his pot belly. Lulizen slowed and looked round, "is this true?"

"Yes. Please come to the audience chamber." One of her maids pleaded, "he will arrive soon." She clasped her hands in hope and looked at Lulizen fearing that her nineteen-year-old charge would run off again like a disobedient child.

Lulizen reluctantly let them lead her to the women's section of the audience chamber where there was a brazier in one corner with dried herbs burning on the charcoal. She sat down on her cushioned stool beside the rest of her family and a selection of court women. She glanced through the spaces of the ebony screen while her maids fussed over her hair and clothes. Her long silky black hair was quickly re-plaited before being pinned into a bun close to the nape of her neck with several silver pins.

She wore several layers of satin and brocade silk with wide sleeves. Each layer was done up with small buttons. The waist length jacket on top was quilted against the cold mountain air. The maid moved the skirts so the embroidered mountains and clouds could be seen. Her mother tutted and frowned at the quilted slippers that were looking frayed from her outdoor running.

Lulizen shifted uncomfortably in her court clothes. She preferred her riding clothes of a silk blouse and baggy woollen trousers with a warm fur-lined coat over the top and calf length boots with long laces. She rode to escape the formalities of her father's court, riding on her hairy sturdy mountain pony down the narrow mountain paths. She rode with just one guard in attendance and was allowed to go wherever she wanted apart from one narrow steep-sided valley shrouded in cloud. It was here that it was told dragons lived.

She tucked a wisp of hair behind her ear and re-adjusted the necklace she wore that lay between her plump breasts. Her leg and arm muscles were taut from all her riding. Her tanned face was round and had beautiful brown almond shaped eyes as well as a small nose. When she smiled dimples appeared in her cheeks.

Looking through the latticed screen she could see the whole of her father's audience chamber with its carpets and rich hangings of mythical beasts. Her father, the Lord of Gloabtona, sat wrapped in gold brocade, hiding the plain quilted jacket underneath which in turn hid his fat stomach from too much feasting. His flat topped headdress hid short cropped grey hair. His eyes appeared half closed but they were sharp and alert to everything going on around him.

To each side of the room sat the male courtiers. By the door stood two soldiers dressed in scaled armour and holding hooked spears, a reminder of a past life connected with dragons though no one remembered what it was. No stories were told of them apart from in fear though no dragons had been seen for years.

A murmur rose up amongst the men and the women all moved closer to their screen. There was disappointment when their visitors turned out to be a lone man. Where was the entourage for who was supposedly an important man? The courtiers whispered to each other trying to work out what was going on. Lulizen couldn't help being curious although she tried to resist.

She didn't quite know what to make of this great lord from a far off land for he certainly didn't look like one. He was dressed simply as if he had lost his luggage and entourage. He wore a large sailcloth coat over a woollen tunic and trousers. His face was tanned as if he spent a lot of his time in the sun. His caramel brown hair, which had a touch of grey within it, was slightly windswept from his journey up the twisting track to the palace. Her mother leant over, "what do you think?"

"Is it true then?" She glared at her mother.

"Is what true?"

"Father wants me to marry him?"

Her mother pretended that she hadn't heard the question and calmly said, "I will speak to your father."

"I have neither agreed nor disagreed to anything." Lulizen protested, "how can you let me marry someone I've never met, none of us have ever met."

Before her mother could reply one of the others hissed, "ssh, something is happening."

Lulizen peered through the screen again. She saw her father stand and bow to the honoured guest.

Every women behind the screen strained to hear what was being said between the two lords. As a seat was brought forth for the guest her mother whispered, "he is a very great man. He rules the lands far to the south of us. He is the Lord of Dragons."

"I thought they didn't exist apart from in myth."

"They do where he lives. Quiet, they talk." Her mother put a finger to her lips.

In the main room tea was placed on a small table between the two leaders.

"I am travelling the lands in search of the missing colonies of dragons. I know you have a valley near here named after them."

"We do your lordship. Do you need help getting there?"

"A guide is all I need and access to your library." The visitor took the tea offered to him.

"That I can do. I have a proposition for you."
The guest frowned, "what is that?"

"I will give you all you need and in return I suggest a union. You are going to need more than a guide and books. Your brother's rule over your lands is growing stronger and you will need my help if you want to regain control of them."
The guest's eyebrows rose, "that is certainly interesting to hear. I have obviously been away too long. So, what union do you propose?"

"My youngest is now of a good age."
The guest chuckled. Obviously this daughter was either unruly or actually getting too old, "do I get to meet this daughter of yours?"

"You can."

"Let me think on this."

"Thank you. My offer is my support for my daughter."

"I will think about it." The visitor said sternly.

"As you wish. Please, enjoy our hospitality. There will be a feast tonight but for now I will get a servant to show you to your rooms." Her father beckoned a servant over.

As the visitor was led from the room he glanced over to the screen. Lulizen sat back feeling as if he had seen straight through the screen and seen her.

The feast came with its many dishes of stewed mountain goat, roasted antelope, steamed vegetables, curded yak cheese and plenty of beer and tea to drink. There were dancers, accompanied by flutes, drums and a singer. The dancers stamped and twirled with delicate movements of their hands and feet, bells rattling at their wrists and ankles. Lulizen couldn't help staring at it all, absorbing it all to remember.

She was rarely allow to attend a feast except for on religious days when the family got together before the court. She looked down the full table to where at the far end of the long table her brother and parents spoke with their esteemed guest. She hoped she might be able to meet him later with or without permission as she still had not been introduced to him.

That night she lay in her bed being indecisive. She wanted to see him close up and speak with him. She didn't want to marry a man that she might not speak to until their wedding day. Should she sneak out or not? Would he be awake or asleep considering how much food had been eaten by all and the journey he had made?

Rolling over she glanced at her maids who were softly snoring on her bedroom floor, before taking a deep breath and making a decision. She slipped out of bed and into a thick night coat to protect against the chill of the mountain night. She slid her door open and shut without a sound. All she knew was that he was in the guest quarters. She moved along the passageways where all the shutters were closed till she came to the occupied suite, the only one with a lamp outside its door.

She took a deep breath again before tapping at the door frame. There was no answer so she risked sliding the door open. The bedroom was empty but the screen into the small private garden was open. It wasn't really a garden, just a small scrap of greenery before there was a cliff edge. She slipped across the room and peered out. She stared in astonishment as she found him lit up by the moon floating cross legged over the patch of grass in just trousers. She whispered to herself, "what are you?"

"Kittal." Came back an answer.

Her eyes widened and she asked, "you heard me?"

"Yes. You must be my intended bride." He returned to the ground carefully uncrossed his legs and landing on his feet. He approached where she stood nervously on the step. Apart from family she had never been so close to a man.

She found herself looking up into his face. At the audience she had only been able to see the side of it so she took advantage now of his close proximity to study him. He looked weathered and there were frown lines on his forehead and wrinkles in the corners of his eyes which hinted at merriment. His grey eyes were half lidded as he studied her in turn. His nose looked like it had been broken and mended slightly crooked. There was also a silvery scar that ran down across his cheek to the corner of his mouth giving his lips a slight sneer. With a hint of a smile he asked, "so what is your name?"

"Lulizen. You can't just be called Kittal? They didn't announce your titles. My father has never bowed to anyone else before."

"At the moment you don't need to know any more then my name. I have not agreed to anything yet. I do not like my hand being forced." He remarked as he walked into his room. She remained at the door as she saw the scars covering his back in the moonlight. He pulled on a robe left for his use as he turned to her, "come in, don't fear me. We may as well talk now rather than under the eye of a chaperone."

"A chaperone?" She asked cautiously as she sat on his bed, "why would we need one of those?"

"Because you are unmarried and I am a stranger in this court."

"Why do you think your hand is being forced?"

"I may need your father's help but it shouldn't be coming with conditions from an inferior lord. And then there is you. I am not interested in having a wife forced upon me. Any more questions?" He sat opposite her on a stool from the dressing table.

"Are there really dragons in the valley?"

"Which one?"

"Ours?"

"Possibly."

She eyed him. He was hiding a lot from her. She had a feeling she wasn't going to get much more out of him either.

"Next?"

She looked at his face but it was revealing nothing. She thought for a moment before asking, "if I was to go with you where would we be going?"

"Far away from here. You can't even see the mountains. It would be near impossible for you to see your family."

"Oh."

"But you will be as free as you want to be."

"Do you want me to go with you?"

"The choice is yours." He looked at her from under lowered lids, studying how she would react. She frowned as she became annoyed with him. Did he want her or not? Reading her thoughts Kittal added, "I have been a long time without a woman. I do not know how safe my home will be if I have to go up against my brother. You wouldn't be my wife either."

"Why wouldn't I?"

"For who I am there is a special ceremony and only then would you be considered my wife. If you came with me you would be free to remain as you are or to become my wife later."

"Oh." She didn't know how to react to that. She stood, "I think I should go."

"As you wish." He let her leave. She glanced back in the doorway. She hoped he would be looking at her. He wasn't.

Back in her bed Lulizen felt thoroughly confused. Did anything he had just said mean anything? Did he want her or was he just seeing something in her and offering her an escape? She lay staring at the ceiling. Freedom, it couldn't really become true could it? But then he talked of danger and dragons. She couldn't get her head round that last one. Did they really exist? What did they look like?

She woke late in the morning and asked her maid as she sat at her dressing table, "what do people think of our honoured guest?"

Her maid eyed her suspiciously while Lulizen tried to appear nonchalant. Her maid replied, "everyone is intrigued. He has gone already."

"Gone?" Lulizen tried to keep her face blank.

"He's gone to Druk'k Canyon. We'll have to wait and see if he returns."

"Do they think he won't return?" She glanced at the maid.

"He didn't exactly look prepared for going into the valley." The maid remarked brightly as she finished Lulizen's hair, "there, perfect."

The maid passed on the conversation to Lulizen's mother who smiled to herself. Just maybe she would see her youngest child married rather than become a spinster and burden on her brother.

Two

    The guide led Kittal to the pass leading to Druk'k Canyon. He began to declare he wouldn't go any further but Kittal waved the protest away. Kittal walked up the pass leaving the guide staring in disbelief. The guide thought Kittal ill-equipped for whatever he was going to find in the mists of the valley. Kittal was wearing the same clothes he had appeared in at court plus a rucksack and appeared weapon less.

    He travelled through the mist, with a hand on the dragon shaped handle of his knife. There was something out there, he could sense it. Heading down the pass into the valley the mist began to clear revealing more of a gorge than a valley. The sides sloped steeply away with a terraced break two thirds of the way up on the left side, while a river ran along the bottom with a narrow piece of land on either side.

    He smiled to himself. Somewhere out there was a mountain dragon and he had a sense it might be the last one. He didn't know how it would react when he came across it. He slid down the loose scree to the riverbank. Now that he was here he had to decide what to do, go search out the dragon or stay put and see if the dragon found him. It was late afternoon so he decided to stay put. He would start exploring in the morning.

    He was sitting by the fire when he felt a wind sweep past over his head. He glanced up, a long shadow briefly blocked the stars. He heard stone bounce down the cliff face as something landed behind him. He looked round and called out, *"I know you are there. Show yourself."*

There was a snort and more rattles of stone as the dragon took off. Kittal returned to the study of the dancing flames of his fire with a smile.

With the morning he scrabbled up the cliff to see if the dragon had left any clue of where he would be found. All he found were the claw marks where the dragon had landed on a small crumbling ledge. He growled in annoyance but took the advantage of the vantage point to look around. The wild dragon had to be deeper inside the valley.

He headed off down the canyon searching for any signs of dragons or of the ancestors to Lulizen's people. He spotted an abandoned nest on the far side of the river. With hope he waded across the river and carefully climbed up to the ledge. A puddle of water sat in the bottom of the nest and the rocks and branches were strewn across the ledge though a part of it had been claimed in the past by a mountain eagle. He checked all the rocks just in case one was an egg he could try and hatch. Nothing.

Returning to the bottom he continued on up the canyon. He began to wonder how anyone could have survived in the gorge considering how barren it was apart from the coarse grass at his feet and a few struggling shrubs in the rocks. A herd of mountain goats noted his presence and watched him walk past.

He turned when he heard the scrabbling of hooves on rock as the goats scattered. The ground shook as a long white dragon with a mane of white fur landed, trapping a goat under one of its clawed feet. Its tail draped around Kittal drawing him closer. It bent its whiskered head down and eyed Kittal out of a half blind eye, *"you are not afraid? Do you know what I am?"*

"I do noble beast."

The dragon snorted, *"you should leave human before I eat you."*

"No. I am Nejus of Dragons. I have been searching for the lost colonies." Kittal stood his ground.

"Well I am the last here nobleman. What do you want?"

"I seek knowledge and blood."

"Ha! You'll find neither here till you prove you really are Nejus. You have persevered so I'll give you one chance before I eat you."

From a pocket of his coat Kittal pulled out a bracelet made of copper coloured beads carved with a swirling pattern which glowed as he slipped it on to his wrist. With the skin contact he could control how much power he absorbed from what was contained within the beads. With his hands spread wide and crossing his wrists he sent waves of healing towards the dragon's misty eye. The eye blinked and became clear. He sneered, "ha! Now I can see you, have this." The dragon spat ice at Kittal who rose higher into the air to get out of the way. As the dragon tried again he slammed his hands together and a fireball exploded from them.

The dragon roared and took off. His tail swept towards Kittal. He grabbed the tail as it came towards him. The dragon whipped its tail sending Kittal flying into the air. He somersaulted forward and landed on the dragon's back with a grunt as the landing took the breath from him. For a moment he felt his age and that he was too old for the acrobatics of a Suwar, a dragon rider and warrior.

He lay flat along the dragon's knobbly back and carefully inched forward till he reached the dragon's mane. It twisted and tried to snap at the man. Kittal dug his hands through the mane to the soft skin underneath where he knew there was a nerve he could use to paralyse the dragon.

The dragon began to fall. Kittal leant in close to the dragon's ear, "now listen to me if you don't want to die. I am your Nejus and you have underestimated me. I don't want to tame you. All I want is information. Do you understand me?" The dragon stiffly nodded. Kittal slowly released the nerve and the dragon beat its wings just before they would have both hit the ground. The dragon soared upwards before landing on the terrace in the cliff in front of a cave. Kittal slid off the dragon's back as the dragon growled, *"what do you want?"*

"As I said before, knowledge and blood."

"Go on then."

"The dragon warriors who left. What happened to them?"

"Ha. Some stayed while others moved on. We didn't like the intrusion and fought them off. With no dragons of their own left they departed this valley and set up home in that pleasure fortress of theirs. We tried to rid us of the human scum but instead we found ourselves falling under their weapons. I am the last."

"And what happened to those who left?"

"We heard they found an island."

"I have visited it. It is a place where man rules over the dragons rather than lives alongside them."

"You are the same. You have made them your rides." The dragon sneered.

"But they are free."

"Ha."

"So, you are the last?" Kittal asked.

"Yes. But come with me." The dragon led the way into the cave.

Kittal cautiously followed, a hand on his knife. It took a moment for his eyes to adjust to the dim light. They went deep into the cave which gently sloped downwards. The end of it opened out into a large cavern. Around the edge were several empty nests. The dragon led the way to the only one that didn't look abandoned. Inside the nest sat two eggs. The dragon looked at Kittal, *"me and these two."*

"How long have you had them?" Kittal crouched down and reached out. There was life within them, but it was too cold for them to hatch. Obviously when there had been more of them it would have been warm in the cave, warm enough to hatch eggs.

"Long enough to know they won't hatch here."

"There is still life in them."

"You wanted blood?"

"My colony needs some fresh blood to mix with theirs."

"They are not pure?" The dragon sneered.

"They are mainly savannah and desert dragons who have been breeding together for a long time." Kittal remarked as he ran his hands over one of the eggs. His own had blood of the cliff dragons that used to inhabit the coastline.

"Take them."

"You would be welcome too." Kittal looked up at the ancient beast.

"No." The dragon said sternly, *"I am too old for change. Take them. Just make sure they know where they have come from."*

"I will." He replied as he pulled his rucksack round to put the two large eggs in it.

The dragon didn't try to stop him as he headed out of the cave into the evening light. He decided to stay the night and made a fire just inside the mouth of the cave. Deep in the cave the ancient dragon watched with slow blinking eyes. His job was now done and now he could die.

With the dawn Kittal couldn't sense the huge creature anymore. Leaving the bag in the cave entrance he returned to the cavern. The dragon had turned to dust overnight.

It was three days before he reached the top of the canyon's pass. He had spent the first day working his way down from the terrace. A few times his foothold crumbled leaving him hanging by his fingertips. It was at these points he wished he had his dragon ride with him. If he had he would be on his way home by now. He sighed with relief when he reached the canyon's floor.

Reaching the top of the pass he was surprised to find a group of soldiers trying to build up the courage to venture into the narrow valley. They looked just as surprised. Their leader exclaimed, "we feared you lost."

"What you actually mean is your master feared losing the chance to foist his daughter on me." Kittal glared.

"Sir?" The soldier looked confused.

Kittal rolled his eyes, "never mind. Lead the way back to the palace then."

"Did you find what you were looking for sir?" The soldier attempted to make polite conversation.

Kittal scowled as an answer. The fact that this man's ancestors had helped destroy the Mountain dragon population didn't help.

It was with relief that he sunk into a cotton lined wooden tub full of hot water. Several people could sit in it but currently he was the only one in it. The two bath maids came and went with buckets of hot water. Often they helped the bath occupants clean themselves but they hung back this time, a little afraid of the visitor with his scars.

His limbs ached from fighting with the Mountain dragon and the amount of climbing he had done. When the bath maid approached with a cleaning cloth he gestured for her to leave. He wasn't interested in any female company. His mind was on his own lands and his family, both human and dragon. It was time to go home but first he needed to look through the library.

The bath maids hurried over with a towel and a fur lined robe as he stood. He allowed one to dry him before he slipped into the robe the other held. Stiffly he ordered, "bring me something to eat and drink in the library."

"Yes sir."

Lulizen sat in the doorway of her room with the door half closed, hiding her from the guard that patrolled with a dense furred fluffy maned chow-chow. She was wrapped in a quilted blanket against the cold but at least the open door let the smoke of her brazier out. Opposite her room at the far side of the courtyard was one lonely lamp shining bright. She knew the mysterious lord was in the library. Did she dare walk across to him? She wondered if he had found any dragons.

Everyone was asleep so no one stopped her as she slipped round to her father's library. She stood just inside the room. Her potential husband was knelt before one of the low tables slowly turning the pages of a book. Beside him was a half empty bottle of watered wine and an empty plate apart from the core of an apple.

"Don't skulk in the doorway. Come in or leave."

"How?" She hadn't seen him look over.

"What do you want?" He demanded.

She crept closer and knelt down.

"Why does your father want me to marry you?" He didn't look at her.

She shifted on her knees uncomfortably. She adjusted her blanket around her, "I don't know. I'm not the best behaved. My sister is better at being a lady then me."

"So you don't fit in here."

"I'd rather be out on my pony; free of the court."

He turned and looked at her, "what do you want to do then?"

"Isn't this your decision?"

"Currently I don't care either way."

"What you said the other day, is that still true?"

He nodded.

"Then I will obey my father."

"Do you have anything to wear other than your dresses?"

She frowned at the strange question, "my riding clothes."

"Very good. Be wearing it under your court dress when the ceremony happens. Now, if you'll excuse me, I must finish this book."

She bowed and reluctantly left. The tone of his voice didn't allow any chance to ask questions about Druk'k Canyon.

Three

The ceremony was hastily arranged though her father had not actually heard her agree, just that she had liked the look of Kittal. Now, here they were. Both Lulizen and Kittal sat uncomfortably in front of the priest, both wearing white with Lulizen's parents knelt to one side. Lulizen had a veil over her head, hiding her face from everyone. Only once they were married would a groom see his bride's face. She shifted as her riding clothes were uncomfortable under her borrowed bridal layers

A breeze blew through the paper flower garlands that hung around the open octagonal summer house, its sides temporarily taken down to allow the shivering court gathered outside to look in. The sun was at its height. The ceremony was coming to an end and the bride and groom were holding hands, held in place with a strip of red silk.

The priest was wearing the daftest piece of headgear Kittal had ever seen though he did not say so. Feathers of a condor hung off what looked to be a skullcap. The man stood over the couple and placed his large hands on their heads, "may the Gods bless this couple. May they have a long life and many children to look after them in old age. May they remain healthy and wise. If illness befalls them let each care for the other. Bless them with wealth and knowledge and understanding."

"Amen." Everyone called out.

"You are now married." The priest smiled.

Lulizen bowed her head feeling suddenly shy. For now the man sat beside her was her husband. Excitement was also growing in her, soon she would be free and not really married. Soon she would be going on an adventure that was going to last a lifetime. Out of the corner of her eye she glanced at Kittal through the fine fabric of her veil. His face was revealing nothing.

"Time for feasting." Lulizen's father announced cheerfully as he stood, leaning on a servant.

"I am sorry." Kittal interrupted the happiness saying is so quietly that it was nearly only Lulizen that heard the words. Her father stared down at Kittal in puzzlement, "what do you mean?"

"I thank you for your hospitality but if what you have said is true then I must return to my lands and reinstate my rule."

"Not even for a little while?" Lulizen's father looked as disappointed as a little boy who had been promised a big present that never appeared.

"I am sorry." Kittal got to his feet.

"Of course. You have lands to take care of just like myself." Lulizen's father reluctantly remarked.

"Thank you. Come Lulizen." Kittal held out a hand to his bride.

As she was led from the summer house Lulizen looked back. Everyone was bowed down. With wide eyes she looked up at Kittal's face. Never had she seen her whole family bow down to anyone. She whispered in awe, "who are you really?"

He ignored her question, "ready to go?"

"Yes. The maids almost caught me."

"Good. We'll sort out new clothes for you when we reach home. Now, please be quiet as I need to concentrate."

He led her through her home to a half abandoned smaller courtyard garden. No one was around as they were all attending the feast. They had passed briefly through his rooms to retrieve his rucksack and discard the ceremonial clothes they both wore. He approved of her entire while she stared in amazement. He was dressed in a long sleeved plain tunic held in place by a sash over trousers. He tucked his knife into his sash.

In the garden he pulled out his copper beaded bracelet and held it bunched in his hand. His hand began to glow as Kittal drew a rectangle in front of him forming a doorway in the air. He may be able to create these portals but he couldn't control where they took him. Lulizen looked at the doorway and then at Kittal. With a bow and gesture he said, "after you my dear."

"What do I do?"

"Just walk through it. I'll be right behind you."

Lulizen studied the portal, white against the greenery of the garden. She gulped and shuffled closer to the door. She reached out to the whiteness and felt nothing. The air shifted around her outstretched hand. With another gulp she stepped right up to the portal. She closed her eyes and stepped through. She kept her eyes closed until she felt Kittal's hand on her shoulder and slowly she opened them, fearing what she would see.

Lulizen wasn't sure where to look first, at the dried out lands before her or at Kittal. His face seemed to glare into the middle distance. Around them the land was parched. Dust devils whirled away in the wind. The grasses were brown and brittle underfoot. The trees were withered and skeletal and drained of colour from the winds. Cautiously she asked, "is it normally like this?"

"No." He crouched down and touched the ground, "I've never seen a drought this bad. My brother has not been doing his duty and appeasing the gods." He glanced up at her and then returned his attention back to the soil, "we need rain now."

Just catching the words she looked upwards and wondered how he was going to create rain out of a cloudless sky. Looking down she found him now knelt on the ground and had made a small hole in the ground. From his bag he had brought out a glass bottle filled with a green liquid. He poured it into the ground. He waved his hand over the hole and murmured a request.

They both looked skywards. Clouds were beginning to slowly form. There was a clap of thunder startling Lulizen who hadn't expected it. Beside her Kittal quietly said, *"as you wish."*

Lulizen looked on in horror as Kittal pulled out his knife and calmly cut into the palm of his left hand. He turned his hand and allowed the blood to drip off and into the damp hole. Solemnly he wrapped his hand up as raindrops began to fall. She exclaimed, "why did you do that?"

"The Brothers demanded it otherwise they wouldn't let it rain." Kittal replied as he cleaned his knife and returned it to its sheath, "we must start walking now. Tania will be coming to meet us." He picked up his bag and started walking. Lulizen followed behind.

After a three hour's walk Lulizen was feeling exhausted and hungry, her feet aching in heeled riding boots and the gentle rain had soaked through the silk and wool of her riding attire making her feel heavy. She wondered why they were walking as well. If he was such an important man then why was he not being carried or being met by his court?

Though she was tired she couldn't stop looking around in amazement. Everything was rapidly turning green and even beginning to bloom. It was as if the plants had all been waiting for the rain. She watched Kittal crouch and thought the flower bent towards him as if bowing to him before he plucked it.

She was beginning to wonder how Kittal was not tired and hungry himself when he came to a stop. She barely noticed the hand signal he gave and bumped into him. She received a glare from him and took a step back. With a sigh of relief that they were stopping she sank to the ground to give her feet a rest. She watched in confusion as he knelt down and put an ear to the ground. He listened for a few seconds, looking thoughtful. Standing he said, "get out of the way of the riverbed now!"

"What riverbed?" She exclaimed. Without replying he grabbed her by the arm and dragged her to her feet and up the bank, away from the dry riverbed.

Once far enough away he turned round. Lulizen turned. It started as a trickle and then seconds later with a roar a large wave of water swept by, pouring over the channel's banks. Lulizen stared in astonishment, to think that she could have been taken away with it. She stuttered as the sound faded and the water settled in its bed, "how did you know?"

"Here, in this land, everyone is much closer to nature than you are, many of you have forgotten what it is like to be close to her. Nature in all its elements must be respected." He looked solemnly at Lulizen and she looked grateful for being saved. Feeling suddenly uncomfortable he said, "we still have far to go."

As they started walking again Lulizen asked, to distract herself from her sore feet, "who is Tania?"

"My daughter."

"Where is she?"

"Hopefully making her way to us."

"And her mother?" Lulizen warily asked, wondering if she was about to become a submissive second wife in a foreign harem.

"Dead." He answered bluntly.

"So I am your second wife? How old is she? Why didn't you mention any of this before?" She stopped and demanded.

"You didn't ask and I chose not to say." He replied while still walking, "such information wasn't necessary."

"Not necessary?!" She protested, "I am to be a stepmother to a woman who is possibly older than myself."

He stopped and turned to her and snapped, "yes she is older than you and currently would not be behaving as you are now."

She stepped back, feeling the sting in his words and look.

"Can I remind you that you are not my wife here and also you chose to come with me. You can stay right here if you want." He turned away and started walking.

She had brought up memories he preferred not to remember. He had once loved his first wife until he discovered that she was a manipulative bitch. Her death had left him bringing up a two year old Tania. And they were memories he enjoyed thinking of. For so long it had been just the two of them. But now it would be three and he didn't know how everyone would handle it, including himself.

He hadn't appreciated being foisted into the marriage but having thought about it while walking the mountain valley he had come to realise Lulizen might be the one to give him his much-needed heir. He could only wait and see if she really wanted freedom as her own woman or whether she would be interested to become his wife and a mother. He smiled to himself. He liked her daring already.

Behind him Lulizen glowered at his back even though she was also blushing. She hadn't meant to offend him, but she hadn't known he had been previously married. Her mother had been vague over information on him as if no one really knew who he was apart from having control of dragons. The librarian hadn't told her anything, saying she didn't need to know. It was almost like they were all afraid of him. What had she let herself into? What happened to his first wife? She gulped as she wondered if he was a violent man though there was no suggestion of it from him. Then there was his daughter. What would she be like?

She realised then that he was getting further away from her. She knew she wouldn't survive in this land without him. She had never suffered any hardships. She ran to catch up with him, calling out, "wait, stop… Please."

Kittal stopped and she almost walked into him again. As she tried to catch her breath she said, "I'm sorry."

He responded gruffly, "hmpfh, just keep up."

Lulizen began to slow down again. He softened and swept her into his arms. She put her arms around his neck and leant her head against his shoulder, closing her eyes from tiredness. She found herself feeling strangely safe in his strong arms and it had been a long day.

Although she was light in his arms Kittal was glad to see their destination for the night, a freshwater pool surrounded by trees. Earlier in the day it would have looked dead but now it looked inviting. And what was even better was the sight of his daughter. He forced his tired legs to move faster. He ignored the brief image of his first wife that flashed up as Tania smiled at him across the distance.

Tania ran to her father and fought the desire to jump into Kittal's arms when she saw he was carrying a young woman. She exclaimed in joy, "father!" And then added with concern, "who is this?"

"Lets get to the trees. This is Lulizen." He smiled softly at his daughter.

She led the way and let him place Lulizen on the ground.

They were embracing when Lulizen woke up. She silently watched as Kittal kissed Tania on the forehead. She saw a pair of laughing eyes in a long face, so different from her father's. Tania's plaited hair was a similar shade to Kittal's. She wore a wide sleeved linen blouse tied at the throat. It was tucked into a long skirt behind a wide belt with a knife and small bag hanging from it. On the collar were a few embroidered grape vines.

Tania stopped laughing when she saw that Lulizen had woken up. She eyed the young woman up and down, "where did you find her?"

"Her father proposed a joining in exchange for his support. What has my brother been up to?" Kittal asked as he put his rucksack on the ground.

"You married her?" Tania couldn't believe what she had just heard.

"Only in her father's lands. For now, until she decides what she wants in her life, she is our guest."

"Of course." She sat down next to Lulizen and gave the young woman a warm smile, "welcome to the family. Do you know, it will be nice to have another woman to talk to. Sometimes father can be difficult to speak to as he has so much to worry about."

Kittal pretended not to hear his daughter as he set about making a fire.

The two young women came and joined him by the fire. In the flickering light of the orange flames Tania noticed Kittal's bandaged hand. She moved to her father's side and said, "don't tell me the Gods wanted blood." She unwrapped the bandaged and touched the tender cut. Kittal commented, "it was only a few drops and this place needed the rain." Tania didn't say anything as she found a pot of cool ointment in her own pack and rubbed it into the cut on Kittal's hand. Finishing she said, "this will have to do as I didn't bring a needle. There, don't do it again or it will never heal."

"Their demands must be met."

"There are other ways, like a good drop of wine." Tania pointed out.

"I don't always carry wine with me." Kittal replied looking slightly annoyed that his daughter was telling him what to do. He wrapped the bandage back round his hand as he got to his feet and wandered away from the fire.

While Tania searched through her pack to find food for them to share, Lulizen watched Kittal head away from them. Nervously she asked, "what's he doing? He isn't leaving us is he?"

"He'll be going to mediate and become one with the earth. He has always done it. It calms him as he has a great many things on his mind to worry about. It's the only chance that he can become at peace with himself." Tania informed Lulizen and then asked, "what clothes did you bring?"

"Only these." Lulizen was surprised that Tania was showing an interest in her, "they are my riding clothes."

"What do you ride?"

"Horses. We have small ones in the mountains."

"Tell me about it. I have never travelled anywhere far. I only hear of the outside world from father and my aunt."

"Well," Lulizen settled closer to the fire, "us girls are under strict control. We don't normally have any freedom. Riding was the one concession for me which I was grateful for. I lived in a large house with a garden at the centre of it. We used to have to sit behind screens. I was expected to marry whoever my father wanted. What does your home look like?"

"You'll see." Tania answered as she poked at the fire.

"Does Kittal always rise into the air when he mediates?"

"You have seen him?" It was Tania's turn to be shocked. Lulizen nodded and hoped for an answer, but Tania chose not to say anything. Instead she asked, "is it true that you are married to him like he said?"

"In my law we are but he says we are not so with your laws."

"As you have come with him what do you plan to do?"

"I don't know." Lulizen admitted, "he has said I can stay with him until I have decided."

"He said." Tania remarked quietly as she studied Lulizen, the slight petite young woman who her father had brought back with him. She couldn't decide what she thought of Lulizen. She looked tough but she looked delicate as well, especially with her small feet. Tania wondered how well Lulizen would survive. It was obvious she had been brought up being served upon but now there would be none of that. Only her father had anyone to serve him directly.

Four

Kittal watched over them as they slept. He couldn't sleep though he wanted to. His daughter had updated him on what had been happening while he had been away. He was relieved to hear his uncle had chosen not to take any side between his two nephews. He clearly thought himself too old to leave his home and his wife and many concubines. His uncle had always been a strange one.

It seemed that Titan had been growing stronger and consolidating his rule as no one had known where their anointed ruler was. He had ignored the Gods for the praise and desire of man. It sounded like he had allowed his advisers to encourage him in claiming all but the title of Nejus. That he had struggled with as the dragons had remained loyal to their wandering Lord. It appeared he was going to have a fight on his hands to reclaim his lands.

As for the drought that had crept up on the lands of Keytel until it was too late and when Titan had tried to appease the Gods they had ignored him. The nomads had stopped travelling as there was no longer anyway of sustaining themselves. They settled below Titan's castle and became his army, helping him claim towns and cities.

The only place they didn't venture was Kittal's Valley of Dragons. They didn't trust the dragons so that was Kittal's saving grace. The Valley and its nearby town of Linyee were where his loyal supporters could be found.

He must have dozed off as he was woken by Tania shaking him awake, "come on, time to head off."

"Where are we going?" Lulizen asked as father and daughter pulled on their rucksacks.

"Home." Tania smiled at her.

"Where exactly is that?"

"The Valley of Dragons where my father is Nejus."

"Nejus?" Lulizen asked, beginning to feel embarrassed by the number of questions she was asking.

Tania didn't seem to mind as she linked arms with Lulizen, "his full name is Nejus Kittal, Lord Defender of the Dragons and overlord of the lands of Keytel which my uncle has been regent of for the last three and a half years."

They lapsed into silence. Tania eventually broke away and joined her father who was walking ahead of them. He glanced behind to make sure Lulizen was alright as Tania remarked, "you've been away too long."

"I am sorry."

"Did you find any more dragons? Any Suwars?"

"I did." Remembering some of what he had seen sent a shiver up his back.

"And?"

"Those ancient warriors made their way to the mountains where they came to fear dragons. Lulizen is from those groups and I think there is a little of that original spirit in her."

"Any wild dragons?" She took his hand and held it tight. She felt there was more behind his words.

"One, watching over the last two eggs of its kind."

"And you have the eggs?"

"Yes. They are just waiting for the right moment to hatch. It was cold enough to make them dormant." He replied.

He decided that for the moment he wouldn't talk of the island to his daughter. What he had seen and done had affected him physically and mentally. One thing he knew was that the dragons of the island of Jukirla needed rescuing from their human captors. Never had he thought that Suwars would turn into abusers of their noble beasts. They had forgotten all it was to be a Suwar.

He had been a prisoner himself for a year when they realised he could speak to the dragons. They hadn't liked the idea he might free the dragons from their chains. It was while he was there that he had received the scars on his back. They had put him to work in one of their mines until he managed to escape with one of their dragons who died of its injuries when they reached safe land.

Seeing that her father had retreated into himself Tania left him to his thoughts. Though she wanted to know what he was thinking she knew that he would not react well to her asking. He would talk when he was ready.

She returned to Lulizen's company. While father and daughter had been walking ahead Lulizen realised that Tania, unlike her father, was walking barefoot. She asked, "how can you walk so long without rest and with no shoes?"
Tania shrugged her shoulders, "I have always walked everywhere. There is no other way of getting around unless you are a privileged one and are allowed to ride the Dragons. I've never felt any need to put on shoes and I like bare feet."
"Don't they hurt?"
"I've got tough feet though at first they hurt. He had to wrap them up most nights before they toughened up. They are horrible to look at." Tania commented cheerfully.
"Is he, Kittal, always like this?" Lulizen asked quietly.
"Like what?"
"Serious, solemn, quiet."
Tania was thoughtful before replying, "give him a chance, he's always like this when we first re-unite. I suppose I remind him a lot of my mother."
"Do you remember her?"
"No." Tania said sadly. Brightening up she replied, "I wouldn't mind you though, but you must stop asking question they will annoy him. He knows when you need to know."

After that they fell silent. Lulizen wondered whether Kittal actually did want her as his wife. The thought scared her. Tania looked at Lulizen and asked, "everything alright?" "Yes... I think." Lulizen replied with a smile. She fell silent again as she wondered what it would be like in bed with an older man. All she knew was what the young maids giggled about when making her baths. She guessed that he was in his late forties. A shiver of disgust ran down her back. Tania saw it and asked again, "Are you sure you are fine?"

"I'm fine, honest," she gave Tania a tight smile.

It was late afternoon and Lulizen's feet were so swollen that her boots felt like they might split. She had never walked so far in her life. She regretted it as soon as she moaned, "is there no other way of getting around? How much further?"

Kittal, none too kindly, commented, "unless a herd of wild horses appeared then there is no other way. Do you think a herd will appear?" He gestured out over the greening expanse.

"No." Lulizen replied mournfully.

"Then don't moan I don't like it any better than you do." Kittal snapped before Tania could take control of the situation. Tania took hold of her father's arm making him look towards her. She murmured to him so Lulizen didn't hear, "if you want her, then you are doing a good job of losing her. Be nice to her."

Kittal scowled and then sighed, "I just want to get back to the valley before the day is out."

"We will." Tania said in her normal voice, trying to give her father encouragement not to lose faith just yet, "we can already see it." She pointed ahead of them.

"It has been my one worry while I've been away."

"It is the one place uncle has not dared enter. He knows the valley is too loyal to you father." She gave his arm a squeeze and smiled at him.

Ahead of them, growing in size, was a sight Kittal had been looking forward to. Out of the flat land rose rocks, the two sides of his valley home, which descended into the ground forming a wide basin that had once been the crater of a now long extinct volcano. The drought had not affected the valley but it didn't stop him from offering up thanks to the Gods for looking after his home while he had been gone.

Lulizen couldn't believe how alive the place was. Behind her the plains were slowly coming back to life but the animals remained within the valley's sphere of influence. Kittal was ahead of the women. When they reached the valley entrance he ordered, "gather seeds and scatter them to help life return to the plains."

Obeying the two women began to gather seeds, picking ripe fruit and pulling the grass seeds off the plants and the three of them scattered them outside the valley's shadows luring the animals, birds and insects back out into the plains.

With a brush of his hands together to remove any last seeds Kittal chivvied the two women along, saying, "not long now."
He gave them both a warm smile. Now that he was back in his rightful place, in the valley that was opening out ahead of him, he put his worries temporarily to one side.

His excitement bubbled over on to Tania who skipped along like a little girl, picking flowers and pointing out animals to Lulizen who just stared in wonder. She couldn't believe that the place could sustain so many creatures. Tania excitedly did point out, "you haven't seen the best yet, the dragons." She ended hissing before bursting into a plea of laughter at the sight of Lulizen's worried face, "they won't hurt you, as long as they know you aren't trespassing. There are laws to be remembered though for they are most decidedly wild even if they don't appear so with father or Canaan."

"Canaan?"

"Father's servant, he is wonderful with the dragons even if he is a bit clumsy. He is such a nice person, wait until you see him and then you'll understand." Tania replied, smiling as she thought of Canaan with his kind, inquisitive hazel eyes and the mad mop of brown hair on his head. He had such gentle touches as well, when he held her in secret, just thinking about it made her feel all warm inside. Embarrassed by her silence reminisces, especially as such events were going to be fewer now that her father was back; she gave Lulizen a smile and skipped ahead to pick another flower to add to her growing bunch.

Kittal was far ahead of them, stopping occasionally to examine a plant or harvest it if he thought it would be of use. He knew all the plants that grew in his 'garden' and knew which ones he could use and which ones he couldn't. He glanced back at the pair occasionally but didn't demand anything out of them, leaving them be. He did stop to look down in the stream, which flowed by the side of the path. He looked worried until a silvery fish flickered in and then out of view with a flash of colour on its scales from the light, and he smiled.

As they finally entered the valley there was a pair of stone dragons, wings spread above their heads, meeting in the middle. They sat there looking proud with a scowl on their reptile snouts. The hind claws clung tight to the stone pedestals. At the feet of the one on the left sat a large egg as life like as the rest of it.

Each scale on their bodies was shown on the carved stonework. Staring up at them Lulizen was in awe; so this was what a dragon looked like, not at all like those embroidered on to her court clothes. They looked more frightening and threatening. She shivered from the uncertainness of the beasts and the fear that they might try and eat her on first sight.

When Kittal passed by them the one on the right rose into the air with a flap of its wings. Lulizen stopped in her tracks amazed that such a large creature could rise into the air with such ease. Tania had noticed the dragon rise into the air and knew that it was off to alert Canaan of their return. She walked on not realising that Lulizen had stopped. Seeing how at ease father and daughter were with the dragon she hurried onwards, not wishing to be left behind.

The cool breeze that had been with them out on the plains dropped away. Lulizen felt the change in temperature and then the odd smell wafting towards her. She wrinkled her nose at what smelt like rotting eggs. Coming round a corner in the path a bubbling hot pool appeared, springing from a vent in the ground close to the valley's high cliffs. She wasn't sure whether to believe her eyes as she saw a young dragon playing and bathing in the hot spring. It was enjoying itself so much that it didn't even notice the three people walk by. After that it cooled down again when a breeze appeared as the valley widened out.

Rounding another corner, a house came into view surrounded by a large green lawn. Peacocks strutted around. The house was all one floor with a gentle sloping roof of red clay tiles. A veranda ran round all four sides. The shutters of all the tall windows were open, allowing light and air to sweep through the rooms inside.

At the top of the steps leading to the veranda, in front of the double open doors to the house was a young man in his early thirties, Canaan. He waited patiently for the three of them to reach him. Climbing the steps to Canaan Kittal acknowledged the man's bow with a remark, "I have been too long from here Canaan. It's good to be back."
Kittal handed his rucksack to Canaan, "go gentle with that. Are there any dragons sitting on eggs at the moment?"

"I am pleased to see you back Nejus."

"Speak up my dear boy." Kittal said brightly, giving Canaan a smile, "how have they all been? I noticed Kite fly up from where she was watching."

"Old Narl died Nejus." Canaan replied.

"Yes I remember." Kittal said thoughtfully as he headed into his house, closely followed by Canaan. As Lord

Defender of the Dragons he was so closely linked to them that anything dramatic affected him. While on his travels at the time the last dominant male had died he had fainted away to then come round several hours later knowing that the ancient dragon had gone. "who won the battle? Tyke had the strength, but I know that clever Lupe could have out manoeuvred the bold Tyke."

At this Canaan looked worried and said in a voice hardly above a whisper, "they were equal and decided to both be dominant males."

"What?!" Kittal exclaimed, turning on Canaan with a look of complete shock, "did you try to talk them out of their madness?"

Cringing Canaan replied, "they wouldn't listen. I didn't know enough words to put it across."

"Bring them both here. I'm not having this, it isn't right." Kittal ordered angrily before sweeping into what was the living room, sunken into the ground. Cushions were scattered across wide ledges that acted as seating. Around the walls were potted green ferns, giving the room a sense of being outside. He dropped on to a pile of cushions scowling. Lulizen couldn't help pitying the servant as he quietly slipped out of the room. What she wasn't to know was that that had been the first time Kittal had been angry at Canaan. She glanced at Tania, but she had vanished.

Looking up from where he sat Kittal saw Lulizen standing uncertainly in the doorway. He patted the cushions next to him and said, "please, come and sit, there is no need to hang around over there, you are a welcome guest." Cautiously Lulizen sat down and tentatively asked, "what was all that about?"

Kittal laughed, already forgetting his anger with Canaan. Becoming serious he explained, "when the dominant male dies another must take his place. To get the right one all the males must fight it out through skill and brains. The last two must fight until one or the other admits defeat. It has taken a week before now, neither dragon wanting to lose his pride on it. Old Narl won through brawn. There has never been two dominant males and I'm not letting it start now. Discussions indeed, what next?"

"They can talk?" Lulizen asked in surprise. The stories she had known were where the dragons were all vicious beasts that never had any reason to talk.

"Of course they can." Kittal spluttered, amazed that Lulizen could think any other way, "dragons are very intelligent, some more so than others, but all intelligent. They know more about the world than I do." Looking up he commented to himself more than anything, "where has Canaan got to? They are probably hiding. they definitely deserve a telling off if they are." To Lulizen he said, "if you'll excuse me a moment."

He impatiently walked in and out of the rooms of his home as he waited for Canaan to return. He was about to head outside when Canaan rushed in, "I've found them and they are waiting."

"Good, don't let them disappear, I'm coming." Kittal replied as he headed after Canaan, who had returned outside at a jog. Lulizen followed him curious to find out what a Dragon looked like up close. Tania was already outside and glanced at the pair as they arrived on the green lawn. A few metres away crouched two dragons, twice the size of any of the people standing in the garden. Both of them looked sheepish. Seeing Kittal cross the lawn both bowed their heads and in deep voices said, *"welcome back Nejus."*

"What is this I have heard from Canaan? Two dominate males? I'm going to knock some sense into you two feeble-headed dragons." Kittal said grimly, ignoring the pleasantries. He glared at both of them with his arms crossed in front of him. Behind him Tania whispered to Lulizen before she asked, "it is the language of the dragons. It is a very hard tongue to learn. Father can speak it fully. Canaan knows enough to communicate to them."

Lulizen didn't get a chance to ask anything for Kittal was speaking in the harsh dragon tongue again, *"you are going to do this properly, otherwise I'll throw you both into exile and we'll start all over again."*

"You can't do that." The dirty red Dragon on the left, and the older of the two, protested. His front claws dug into the ground in his frustration

"I'm guessing you are more willing to try my patience than Lupe. I don't want to be sorting your silly mess out minutes after getting back, but it needs to be done." Turning to the dark grey Dragon with two horns on its snout and it rested on three large claws halfway along the length of his wingspan; Kittal continued, *"are you sure you want to go down in history as a Dragon of ridicule, Tyke? Or do you want to be remembered as a brave Dragon that understood when to give in if this is done properly? It is of course your choice."* Kittal shrugged his shoulders as if he didn't care, *"please make your decisions quickly both of you, I do have more important things to do."*

The two Dragons glanced at each other, both knowing that they were going to have to fight. They nodded their scaly heads at Kittal and Lupe said *"we will fight Nejus."*

"Good." Kittal replied with some relief, *"till tomorrow then, prepare yourselves well."*

They gave him stiff bows before spreading their wings and lifting into the air to fly back to nests and mates. Both felt humiliated by the fact that their Nejus had had to have words with them.

With the dragons gone Kittal sighed. He could now get on with other matters such as planning a visit to his brother. To Canaan who stood just behind him he instructed, "you need to make up a bed for our guest, Lulizen, and then sort dinner out. Get some of my tea as well."

Five

Waking in the morning in his soft bed placed in the centre of his bedroom, he still felt exhausted. He stared round his room and smiled, glad to be home after all his travelling. His bed had thin curtains hanging down from a centre point on the ceiling giving him privacy when he wanted it. At the large open windows of his room were wind chimes softly moving in a faint breeze making a soothing tinkling sound. Canaan had placed Kittal's beaded bracelet on his desk in one corner of the spacious room.

Kittal knew he hadn't slept well through the night. It hadn't been the warm night as he was use to that, sleeping naked under a thin blanket. He had spent the night tossing and turning from dreams that had disturbed his sleep. He dreamt of the loss of his valley and the dragons under his care were dead or enslaved.

He rolled out of bed unwillingly and put on the robe Canaan held out for him. Canaan saw the scarred back but said nothing- he would ask Tania later if she knew of them. Kittal tied the robe up as he walked into the living room. Tania looked up from her sewing and commented, "Lulizen is still asleep."

"I'll get dressed." Kittal replied and headed out again with a yawn. He felt like going back to bed.

Sitting down on his bed, he fell backwards on to it, closing his eyes as he did. Canaan woke him moments later saying, "the duel sir."

Kittal moaned but rubbed the sleep out of his eyes. To the younger man he commented, "I'll wear my flying gear under the robe."

"As you wish." Canaan replied as he got out one of Kittal's ceremonial robes and the clothes made specifically for when he was flying Kite. Kittal pulled on the clothes. Over a shirt he wore a padded jacket with sleeves that were wide at the top and narrowed to skin tight from the elbow to the wrist. It had a knee length gathered skirt which kept his thighs warm when flying high in the sky where it was a lot colder than on the ground. For the moment it was only half done up. It was all a pale grey colour, matching Kite's colouring. He tucked his hard-wearing Dragon hide gloves into his belt. Though they were called dragon hide the gloves were actually made of thick but supple leather.

Canaan helped him into a sleeveless robe. It had a pale grey lining and a deep red outer layer. The edges of it were embroidered with vines and on the back an elaborate serpent like Dragon twisted into the sky. Every Nejus of the Dragons had several to wear for when he was performing rituals and ceremonies with the dragons, either reusing old ones or having new ones commissioned.

By the time he was ready Tania had woken Lulizen. Lulizen stared at Kittal as he appeared. What he wore he seemed to look nobler than he had been before. Seeing the twisting embroidered dragon on his robe Lulizen wondered whether her ancestors had come from Kittal's lands. She made a mental note to ask Kittal one day.

She felt drawn to him, but he didn't notice since Tania had given him a bowl of a special tea mixture. He visibly relaxed as he felt the tensions of the day before and the night leave him. He looked at the two women as he finished the bowl and handed it empty to Tania. Canaan had gone to make sure that the two dragons were ready to fight. Returning he said to Kittal, "they are ready sir."

"Lead the way then my dear fellow." Kittal said cheerfully. To Tania and Lulizen he asked, "will you be joining myself and the dragons?"

Tania nodded eagerly and replied for both of them, "of course we will."

As they headed towards the dirt arena, Kittal and Canaan leading the way, Lulizen, dressed in borrowed clothes for the moment, asked Tania with concern, "isn't this a bit barbaric?"

"It is the way it has always been done." Tania informed her, "dragons don't like change so don't try changing our traditions." She glanced at Lulizen to check the other got the warning. Lulizen had understood the warning.

It was only a short walk away and they soon arrived. Under an awning were several chairs, the middle one obviously for Kittal with its many carvings of dragons. The arena space was small for most of a dragon's duel happened in the sky. Around the edge were the hundred or so dragons, which lived in the valley. All of them bowed low to Kittal as he walked under the awning and sat down followed by the other three. Canaan took his place behind his lord as the ladies took a seat either side of Kittal.

Kittal leant on one arm of the chair gazing across the arena into the distance looking thoughtful although he hadn't planned to do any difficult thinking. He had begun thinking about Titan and was wondering what his brother was up to. He forced the thoughts out of his mind and watched, calmly as the two duellists landed. They bowed towards Kittal and then at each other before rising into the air with one flap of their large wings, one after the other.

Slowly they began to circle each other, eying the other as they did, looking for signs of weaknesses. Tyke, the grey horned dragon, was the first to pounce forwards, using the claws on his wings to gouge the red scaled Lupe's unprotected flank. Lulizen gasped as she saw blood ooze out of the deep cuts. Kittal looked at her sternly as if he disapproved of her for make a noise. She put a hand over her mouth and tried not to make another sound. Her eyes remained glued on the combat that was going on between the two dragons. Only the sounds of Tyke and Lupe grunting and growling and the occasional roar could be heard.

Determined that he would win Tyke roared so loud that Tania, Lulizen and Canaan put their hands over their ears to save their eardrums. Kittal didn't seem to be bothered. Tyke then lowered his head so his largest horn was horizontal. He went straight for Lupe who calmly nipped out of the way, slashing into Tyke's vulnerable side with a hind leg. To himself Kittal was heard to mutter, "very clever Lupe, very clever, don't get to uppity yet though, you have a long way to go yet."

Angry that his attack had failed Tyke swooped round with ease and glared at Lupe as he hovered trying to form a new plan of attack. Lupe took his chance and went at the dark grey dragon, his hind legs ready to kick. Tyke appeared cleverer than he looked though and used a wing to swipe the majority of the force of the kick away making Lupe snarl. The remaining force of the kick had done some damage though, making a tear in the stretched skin of Tyke's right wing. Kittal hissed through his teeth, "careful Tyke, if it gets any larger your fight is over."

The fighting continued on for over an hour, each dragon dealing out wounds and bruises to the other. Blood dripped off their scales on to the arena's floor turning it red.

Looking around Lulizen noted that all the watching dragons had expressions of deep concentration on their large snouted faces. Kittal also continued to make quiet comments to himself as if he was making notes for if the duel ended in a draw, though it had never happened, and hopefully never would. Both fighting dragons were beginning to look tired, but neither one gave up, not wanting the other to become the dominant male.

It was Tyke who fell to the ground first, making the ground shake as he landed with a thump. He struggled to his feet, rolling off his back. With a flap of his wings he was up in the air again but Lupe pushed him back to the ground with a well-aimed kick. Tyke struggled up feeling exhausted, but instead of getting back in the air he flattened himself to the ground his torn wings folded over his body. To Lupe he said, *"I can not go on, my wings are too torn to hold me up. You are the true dominant male."*

Both dragons turned to look at Kittal to see how he was reacting to this. He stood and said to them, *"you put on an honourable fight Tyke, but for once brain beat strength and fighting skill. Congratulations Lupe, make sure you are a worthy leader or they may rebel against you. Now get out of my sight the pair of you."*

Obediently the pair rose and flew back to their nests to nurse wounds. The audience followed more slowly, discussing all that they had seen. As Kite turned to go Kittal called out, *"Kite at the house please."*

The dragon appeared to smile and as she rose gracefully she flapped her wings once, then twice before landing on the lawn of the house.

She waited with growing excitement while the four humans walked back to the house. By the time they reached the house Kittal had discarded his ceremonial robe, handing it to Canaan and done up his jacket with its internal buttons. He was now wrapping a turban round his head and face, which would hide all his features once he had finished. He left it partly undone for the time being, until he was in the sky. He entered the house and then shortly re-appeared carrying a saddle and wide girth. Slung over his back he had a large but short elaborately carved bow, top and tailed with the tips of Dragons' tails. Along with it he had a quiver of arrows, which he would attach to his saddle once he had it on Kite.

Kite dropped to all fours, her front limbs claws on her wings, allowing Kittal to get his saddle on to her back. As he tried to get the girth done up he commented with a faint smile, *"you're getting a bit on the plump side my girl and I*

can't have that. Let's have a look Kite; it may finally be your heiress."
She sat up on her hind legs so it was easier for Kittal to have a feel of her belly. As he touched a ticklish spot she guffawed, *"don't, that tickles."*
Looking up at her Kittal said, *"Well my dear, this will be your last flight until that little one cracks through its shell. I'll just have to hope that this girth fits for the time being."*
He gave her belly a rub as he finally got the girth buckled up. With Kite's help he pulled himself up into his saddle which had a high back and front to keep him firmly in, most of the time.

She was eager to take flight with her Lord on her back, but she had to hang on for a moment longer. Tania hurried out of the house calling, "wait." Up at her father she asked, "are you going over Linyee?"

"I can if you want, why?"

"I need some cloth to make Lulizen some clothes."

"I'll see what I can do." Kittal replied cheerfully. With a smile Tania threw up a small pouch of money, which Kittal caught and pocketed. She stepped away as Kite stretched her wings and rose into the air, seemingly taking over the sky as Lulizen stared up in awe. Kittal gave Tania a wave as he guided Kite, with a gentle touch of a knee, in the direction he wanted to go in.

In the air and soaring through the clear skies the whole landscape could be seen. Most of the scenery was the recovering savannah. Far off to the right was the city of Keytelia; which could just about be seen on the horizon, where Kittal's and Titan's uncle lived with his merry harem.

The nearest big town to the valley was Linyee. They flew over was the loyal double walled town which was atop a large tell, layers of past Linyees and its citizens underneath the current one. A wide road led up to a large gatehouse which led into the current town. An abandoned quarter crumbled outside the newer wall when the populace from it moved into the safety the walls gave. Its fortress was currently abandoned.

A long train of camels and horses slowly heading to Linyee through the fields, past the large oasis that watered the area, shied as the shadow of the dragon flew over them. The merchants looked upwards, some in joy and some in awe. It had been too long without their Nejus and his dragon. Titan had ruled well but the two year drought had shown that they had needed the Nejus' return.

With a nudge of his foot Kite flew down low as the merchants grabbed their animals. The youngsters with the group jumped up and down at the thrill of the sight of a dragon. Kittal held up a gloved hand to acknowledge their shouts and bows. They cheered as Kite rose up into the air again. Kite roared and a few horses broke free and galloped off. Kittal laughed.

Already they were leaving the traders behind. Kittal leant over Kite's neck, *"I'm glad to be back. I've been away too long."*

"We have all missed you." Kite replied, *"and I have missed you too. I have missed our flying together."*

"I'm sorry I was away for so long. I didn't plan it that way."

"Did you find any more of us?"

"I did. The cave dwelling desert ones did not want to know. I found the last of the mountain colony and I came back with their last two eggs. I also found an island where they are used as beasts of burden. They are prisoners. As soon as I have reclaimed my authority over Keytel I will be returning to free them."

"Good." Changing the subject she asked out of curiosity, *"who was that girl with you at the duel?"*

"Lulizen. What do you think of her?"

"I don't know, where is she from?"

"The mountains. Her father had me marry her as a condition for a loan of his men. He seemed to think Titan is consolidating his rule and Tania has confirmed it. For now

she is a free woman as you know but I do need an heir."
Kittal became thoughtful, *"Tania can't become Nejus."*
"Why not?"
"It's just not the way it's done." Kittal said with a shrug of
his shoulders. Kite turned her head to look at Kittal through a
large cow like brown eye, *"She seemed nice, not tough
though. Maybe once I've got to know her I could make a
better judgement."* She turned her attention back to her
flying.
"First thoughts?" Kittal asked interested to find out the
Dragon's opinion.
*"I'm not going to object if you take her as a mate. If she
makes you happy then that's what is important. She may not
be interested in you though."* Kite ended with an example of
her wisdom, *"from what I have seen, young women go for
young men. There are only a few that willingly mate with an
older man and that is normally for other reasons like title or
riches."*
"I'll take your thoughts into consideration." Kittal said
seriously.

After several hours of flying a castle came into view
above a river that curved round it. It was a walled fortress
with a large gatehouse dominating the road up to it with a
large square tower on the river side. Another large tower
dominated the other corner topped with a dome.
Fertile fields spread out from the river with small
canals dividing them up, feeding the fields with water. A new
encampment of tents and shacks sprawled along the
riverbank. The previously nomadic tribes stared up as the
dragon's shadow passed over them. They weren't sure
whether to defend themselves or fall to their knees and ask
for forgiveness. They watched as the dragon circled the
castle. They decided to wait and see what happened between
the two brothers first. Men were sent to report back what they
heard.

Above them Kittal said, *"once I'm down get up on to the walls or a tower. I want you as imposing as possible so everyone is reminded of who is the true ruler of this realm."* She nodded as she flew down low enough for him to slide out of his saddle and land with a grunt on the road leading up to Titan's home. He watched her fly up and land on a tower, sending the sentry running as tiles slipped from its roof. He smiled ruefully as he walked up to and through the dominating square gatehouse where banners of his family crest hung down the height of the walls. He unwrapped his turban as he went.

He scowled at a soldier who tried to bar his way and grabbed at the spear. He threw it away from him and the soldier went with it and crashed against the wall. A servant saw what happened and was soon running ahead of Kittal in the hope he could warn his lord of the visitor's arrival.

The servant stumbled into the hall but he was too slow as Kittal marched in behind him. Titan, a plumper version of his brother, jumped from his seat, "Kittal?"

"Brother."

Titan stepped down from his dais and tried to hide his surprise. His group of attendants turned to see what would happen between the brothers. Kittal sneered, "I see you still feel the need to surround yourself with admirers and advisers. Still don't trust your own judgement."

Titan stopped and hesitated before saying, "I didn't know you were back."

"Three days and I am here to thank you for looking after Keytel but now I am back its time for you to step back." Kittal stood taller to dominate his brother.

"Why should I?" Titan grew bolder, "you have no way of stopping me."

"I have the Gods on my side. A two-year drought?! Did you not think to appease the Gods and the Great Dragon Lord?!" Kittal demanded.

Titan didn't bow under his brother's abuse, "the Gods and dragons are the past. It is time for man to rule supreme. I have men behind me."

Kittal raised an eyebrow and sneered, "and how much magic have you had to use to keep them on your side?"

Titan didn't answer. He glared at his older brother.

Kittal felt pressure on his mind and Kittal ordered, "get out of my mind Titan."

Feeling bolder Titan leered, a small evil smile forming as he studied his brother. He had always been able to read the minds of others and he had used it to manipulate in the past. The one mind he had never been able to get into was his brother's but now… now, something had happened to Kittal's that had weakened him mentally just enough to allow Titan in. He fought hard not to reveal what he had briefly seen before Kittal had felt his intrusion. It was certainly something he could use against Kittal. He had also liked the sight of dragons brought down to the level of animals, far removed from the godlike status Kittal kept them in.

Kittal demanded, "step down or feel my wrath."

Titan didn't care now. He had information he could use, "go ahead. You've been away too long and I have control of these lands now."

"Not the important bit."

"Do you know that valley of yours doesn't matter."

Kittal gripped his knife and through gritted teeth declared, "I am Nejus, not you. You will not win." He stalked from the room.

With his brother gone Titan shouted in anger, "why was I not told he was back?!"

No one answered. They all took a step backwards. However much Titan liked to think he was better than his elder brother he was not. There were times when he was more volatile than Kittal, jealous that their grandfather had doted on his older brother and had ignored Titan's own talents. He had the blood of ancient Nejuses in him as well and had some minor power of his own and didn't need some silly vessel to control it either. Titan stamped a foot, "this is my land now. Shoot him down before he leaves."

Someone tentatively piped up, "the dragon?"

Titan swore. Was he surrounded by fools?! He declared, "they are nothing. They are animals and can be killed. Kill them both now!"

Now he needed to decide what to use from the information he had got from his brother's mind.

Outside Kite flew down. Kittal reached out and grabbed her tail. She flung him upwards and he landed in his saddle with a grunt. He decided he was definitely getting too old for such acrobatics. He shouted to her, *"get ready to show them what we are made of."*

"It did not go well?"

"No." He said stiffly.

"This is the Nejus I know and love." Kite remarked eagerly as she climbed upwards.

"Don't exert too much energy. Think of the little one." He cautioned as he put an arrow to bowstring, *"this is just a warning."*

Kite swooped in low and with a deep breath she released a ball of fire at the same time as Kittal unleashed his arrow. The men on the battlements weren't quite sure what to do, having never seen a real fire-breathing dragon before. What was even worse for them was that the dragon had a rider firing arrows at them. An officer came to his senses and shouted at the bumbling soldiers, "fire at it you fools! Shoot it down!"

They were the last words the officer said as a red-hot flaming ball engulfed him, turning him to ashes instantly.

Titan hearing the shouts ran out into the courtyard. He watched as a man fell from the battlements in flames and another with an arrow in his body. He shouted at the soldiers on the battlement who were in disarray, "fire back you fools!"

He grabbed at a soldier who was running past. The soldier nearly fell backwards but quickly righted himself as his lord ordered, "fire arrows at him."

With shaking hands the man put an arrow to his bowstring. The arrow barely reached the top of the walls.

Spotting his brother Kittal smiled and aimed an arrow at him. He could easily kill him if he wanted but chose to sending a warning shot. The arrow buried itself into the courtyard up to its feathers at Titan's feet. He stared at it and then up at the sky. Kittal shouted down, "next time I won't miss on purpose."

With the damage done Kittal turned Kite away with the gentlest of pressure with his knee. She didn't complain as she turned away since she had had more fun than any of the other dragons would ever have. This was one of the few times she could pretend to be wild and not have to worry about the consequences.

Below them Titan's men finally got themselves organised. As one they pulled their bows back and released their arrows. They flew high enough to bounce off Kite's thick scaly skin, sounding like rain on a tin roof. Kittal lay low in his saddle so as not to be hit by the arrows. He patted his dragon's neck and commented, *"excellent work if I may say so."*

"Where now?"

"Home via Linyee."

Six

It was market day at Linyee. The stalls were all in the shadow of the tell the town was on, around the bottom of the road that led up to the town. A few nomads were there selling their wares otherwise it was the townsfolk and some of the farmers.

Everyone stopped in their transactions as the shadow of Kite swept over them. They looked up and in the direction of where the dragon was going to land. Most of them abruptly stopped their negotiations and headed towards the edge of the market where Kite landed and was now scratching her wing with her head. They were curious to see who had arrived on the back of a dragon. Kittal slipped off the dragon's back and gave her side a pat, *"you were great as always."*

The crowd gathered a few feet back from the Dragon and rider, circling them. Many of them hadn't seen a dragon for several years, the younger children never at all, believing that they had only been parts of a story and nothing more. One man stepped from the crowd, the people parting around him to give him space to walk through. Kittal walked towards him unwrapping the cloth from around his face so he could be identified. The brightly robed man from the crowd on recognising his Nejus said, "welcome my Lord. It is an honour to have you once again in our humble town."

"What's all that for councillor? You know myself, my servant and my family have always come here." Kittal said cheerfully.

"We feared you were angry with us since for the past three years only your servant and daughter have come."

"I've been away for a while." Kittal replied.

"Would you care to join myself and my wife for a spot of tea and a smoke of the pipe?" The balding councillor asked brightly.

"Not today, I have business to be done."

"As you wish my Lord." The councillor bowed, "will you need any help?"

"I'll be fine." Kittal said back in the hope the councillor would leave him be.

Getting what he wanted with a large number of hangers-on was not what he wanted but there was nothing he could do about it. Returning to Kite there was a small crowd of children looking at the dragon through wide eyes. They scuttled away as Kittal approached them with the package of cloth for Tania. From their new positions they watched the dragon crouch close to the ground allowing Kittal to climb into the saddle. He ignored the staring children as he said to Kite, *"let's go old girl. We've done enough for one day wouldn't you say?"*

She nodded her large head as she stretched out her wings to rise into the air. The children looked to the sky as they watched the dragon and rider fly westwards. With the object of their attentions gone they ran back to parents who cuffed them round the ear remarking, "you should have more respect for your Lord and the dragon, you don't want to be eaten by one of them."

Back in the valley both women looked up from where they were seated on the veranda as Kite landed on the lawn. Tania put down the dress she was making with a deep breath. Canaan had told her of the scars on her father's back and she needed to know what had happened to him to get them. She called out to him as she crossed the lawn, "father?"

He glanced at her as he undid the girth and then at the parcel on the ground, "hope this is enough for you."

She picked it up, "it will do, thank you." Cautiously she went on, "father, Canaan said you have scars on your back. What happened to you?"

He turned, "we'll talk in my study." He carried his saddle through to his study and put it in its place before sitting down behind his marble topped desk. He pulled out a rolled-up map from a pot containing several rolled up maps. He unrolled it across the desk, putting weights on the corners and stared at it intently for several minutes in silence. Tania waited patiently while standing on the other side of the desk, hugging her parcel.

Looking up at his pretty daughter he sighed. Tania asked, "what is it? What's wrong?"

"Prepare to fight. Titan is not giving up his hold of Keytel." His hand became a fist, "I was away too long."

"We have the dragons."

"He doesn't think he needs them."

"Oh?" Tania sank into a chair. She decided not to bring up the scars, "what do we do?"

"Fight."

"You attacked?" She asked cautiously.

"Just a taster." He smiled as he remembered the exhilaration of soaring over Titan's home on Kite and showing his brother his strength. If only he had had Kite when he reached Jukirla. Maybe he wouldn't have been held as a slave for a year. Changing the subject he remarked, "do you know she has an egg inside her?"

Tania brightened, "she does?"

"Her child will not be for me. Fetch Lulizen, she must be brought round to help us."

"She doesn't know anything." Tania protested.

"I thought you liked her?" Kittal commented with a small smile making his daughter blush in embarrassment.

Lulizen entered the study nervously with Tania behind her who had a serious expression on her face. She glanced at Kittal who looked thoughtful as he stared at the map trying to work out what he should do. He feared what his brother would do with whatever he gleamed from his mind. He turned to look at Lulizen without moving from his position. Seeing her fearful look he commented with a smile, "there is no need to be frightened Lulizen."

He sat back in his chair and glanced outside as Canaan caught his eye, walking by with a basket of harvested fruit from the house's orchard. Turning back he spoke, "Lulizen you must understand that life is different here from where you came from. You may have come thinking you'll be living peacefully here, but that has changed. I must fight my brother to reclaim control of my realm and he will definitely fight back. Considering the dangers that there will be you do not need to stay. I can send you away if you so wish it." He looked at her.

Lulizen looked round at Tania and saw her crossed fingers. Tania remarked, "we are going to need all the support we can get."

"Tania." Kittal said sternly, "don't try influencing her."

"Sorry." Tania replied, bowing her head. She looked at Lulizen hopefully from her lowered eyes. She saw her shuffle in her seat and open her mouth to say something but then shut it. She opened it again and she said, "I don't want to go back to my father's court now that you have introduced me to what freedom could be like. I want to help if I can."

"Thank you." Kittal sounded relieved. "if you want to leave later on I won't stop you."

He stood and came round and gave Lulizen's shoulder a squeeze. He almost went in and kissed her but stopped himself as he wasn't sure of the emotion behind it. He saw her hand tentatively reach up to his and took his own away, suddenly embarrassed. He turned to gaze out of the window as he tried to regain his composure. Turning back, he commented, "it will be hard work, are you ready for it?"

"What sort of hard work?" Lulizen asked eyeing the man, suddenly feeling afraid.

"Learning how to handle and use a sword, staff and bow. You won't be riding a Dragon but you need to be able to defend this place with everyone else."

Carefully Lulizen nodded her head in understanding, "I'll stay still."

It was Tania's turn to get excited as she realised Lulizen was definitely staying. She hugged Lulizen over the back of the chair, pleased with the young woman's decision. Kittal commented, "we have plenty of time to get you up to scratch since I can't do anything until Kite has her heiress."

"Why?" Lulizen asked out of curiosity.

"Her line has always been the ones to fly the Nejus. It takes a year before a new dragon is born, cracking through its shell. Patience is of the essence here." Kittal ended with a deep sigh since he was impatient to be doing things so Titan had no chance to make plans and make the first attack. He would also need to seek out the Suwars led by his sister. Making it clear that the talking was over with he said, "tomorrow we will begin your learning."

He left the two women to do whatever they wanted while he slipped along a narrow path which had not been used while he was gone. At the end of the path was a small gazebo. Wind chimes hung from the open rafters and knocked against each other softly as the small breeze, which blew through the valley, passed through. The ferns grew close up against the flimsy low walls of the place making it look even more like an abandoned building. The place was empty of furniture. The wooden board floor was bare and worn smooth.

With eyes already half closed Kittal settled on the wooden floor, pulling his feet up close to his body. Placing relaxed hands on his knees he closed his eyes and allowed himself to be taken to his private place of peace and calm. It was a place he had created deep in his mind, one where there was nothing to trouble him and nobody could get to.

The garden in his mind was scented by many herbs and flowers. The plants seemed to fight for the gardener's undying attention though they needed none in that imagery world. In the garden was a little girl of about six, Tania, playing and laughing. Then fading into view came Lulizen kneeling in the grass with a basket beside her and in it was a male infant.

In the real world Kittal smiled. He sat there for an hour, so relaxed that he hovered a few centimetres off the wooden floor. He liked the idea of Lulizen presenting him with his much needed heir.

Slowly he opened his eyes, holding a vision of Lulizen dressed in a cream coloured low cut linen dress complimenting her tanned glowing skin, studying him with a gentle loving smile. He knew it could only be fantasy for the time being but he could live with hope that it might happen. He sat for a few minutes not thinking or doing anything before stirring. Getting up he brushed himself down and headed back down the overgrown path towards the house.

Seven

Kittal invited Lulizen on a walk through the valley but when she enquired where they were going she got no answer. Both Kittal and Tania remained mysterious as she was led along a well worn paved path. The path brought them closer and closer to the high cliffs of the valley. Rounding a bend a large mouth of a cave appeared, unusually black against all the greenery and the grey rock face of the valley.

From just inside the cave Kittal picked up a torch and lit it. He glanced at Lulizen to see how she was doing and she gave him a smile as if letting him know she trusted him enough to let him lead her somewhere unknown. Kittal stepped into the cave, the flickering torchlight creating large shadows, which appeared to loom over the three people. The mouth of the cave they had entered through grew smaller and smaller the further they walked away from it. In a nervous whisper, which sounded harsh in the cave's quietness, Lulizen asked Tania, hoping she would get an answer this time, "where exactly are we going?"

"To some of the most loyal people to my father." Tania informed her brightly, "we may look alone in our valley but these are the people that supply us and the Suwars, when they are here, with everything that we need."

Coming out at the other end they walked straight into a village, the prosperous two storey houses surrounded a square with a well in the centre where poultry scratched at the hard packed ground. Children spotted them and recognising Kittal from descriptions their parents had given them of him exclaimed, "the Nejus is here! Lord Kittal is here!"

They weren't sure which way to turn, whether to run to tell everyone else or to head towards Kittal and welcome him. The dogs began barking. Hearing the excited shouting adults appeared in doorways or from round corners of their houses. Realising who it was they forgot all about their work and headed over to Kittal with smiles and, "Lord Kittal it has been too long."

They parted as greying haired Chief Tomas sauntered across from his home in only a pair of trousers. Every glistening inch of his skin was bronze. The Chief and Kittal embraced. Parting, the Chief remarked with a smile, "you have forgiven us then?"

"I was never angry with you, just far away." Kittal explained.

"With successes I hope."

"A few but I'm not here to talk about that. I'd like to introduce you to my guest." Kittal beckoned Lulizen forward, "this is Lulizen from the distant mountain lands of Gloabtona.

"You went that far?" Chief Tomas asked in astonishment while also appraising Lulizen.

"And further."

"Your brother came to illicit our support while you were gone" The Chief remarked as they walked towards his home.

"Did he? I know I have a fight on my hands to regain control of Keytel."

"We are firmly on your side." Chief Tomas reassured.

The Chief's house was also the village's foundry. The whole of the bottom of the building was taken over by his workshop which was open to the square. Up one side of the building was a large chimney stack connected to his furnace where a small fire was burning, idly waiting to be used. A dog lay in front and limply wagged its tail as the group approached.

Sitting just inside, in the shade, was a fifteen year old boy working at shaping a piece of wood, concentrating hard on it. One leg lay in front of him, resting on a stool, twisted as if it had been broken and not healed correctly. He had brown hair and a pair of quiet looking brown eyes. He looked up at the approach of the small group and putting the piece of wood down struggled to his feet, leaning on a crutch which he had had hidden behind him. Kittal looked with concern at the young man and commented quietly; putting a hand on his shoulder, "don't bother."

With a smile of relief the young man sat back down replying, "thank you sir."

Crouching down Kittal asked, "how did you do it Diego?"

"How do you remember who I am?" Diego asked, surprised that the Nejus recognised him.

"How many times did you turn up at the house in the hope that Tania would play with you?" Kittal said with a smile, "you were appearing from the age of five and you had a crush on my daughter. That doesn't matter now though, what happened to you?"

Diego's father answered for his son saying, "he got too close to a dragon. We were both helping Canaan clear some trees. He wandered off. I didn't notice he had gone until both of us heard screaming. We found a young dragon holding him down by one leg, worrying Diego. It crushed the bones in his leg." He looked saddened as he finished the short account of what had happened.

Looking serious Kittal asked, "do you know who it was?"

Shaking his head the chieftain replied, "no, you'll have to ask Canaan."

"I will." Kittal said thoughtfully. To Diego he said, "I'll see what I can do, the dragon will be punished once I have heard his side of the story. What is yours though?"

"I...I..." Diego stumbled over his words, "I know I shouldn't have wandered off, but I did. I think it was trying to play with me but didn't quite understand that it was hurting me. It came from out of nowhere, like it was hiding and was startled."

"I will definitely sort this out." Kittal remarked and then asked, "may I examine your leg?"

"Yes sir."

Kittal moved round to Diego's left side. He knelt down on the ground with Tania peering over his shoulder. Carefully he straightened the left leg out and Diego's face creased in pain. He gasped for breath while Kittal gently touched it trying to get a sense of how much damage had been done. Watching, the chieftain commented, "Katia couldn't do anything. By the time the doctor from Linyee got here he said there was nothing he could do either."
Kittal nodded to show he had heard, but didn't say anything in reply to what the chieftain had said.

He sat back on his heels and rubbed his chin thoughtfully trying to see whether there would be any advantages to breaking the bones and then resetting them to sort out the sorry mess. The members of the group present looked nervous as Kittal took a deep breath to finally speak, "if I had been here at the time I would have been able to do something, it is too late now. That dragon has got away with it long enough. He has ruined the life of someone who could have helped defend the valley." With a sigh Kittal got to his feet. He couldn't find words to say how sorry and annoyed he felt.

The Chief's wife appeared from the back with a tray of clay cups and a jug of watered-down wine and a plate of biscuits. Cautiously she asked, "has he looked?"
The chief sadly shook his head, "there is nothing he can do to it now. It has been too long."

"Oh." She replied with a gulp as he took the tray from his wife's hands. Tania found some more stools and a chair and they all sat down close to Deigo.

With the tray on a spare stool and full cups passed round Kittal said, "what I really came here to do was ask you to make some things."

"What's that then?" The chief asked, curious to know.

"I need armour and a sword made for Lulizen. I need her to be able to defend herself while she lives with us. Titan will probably try everything and anything to keep control of my lands."

"I will be honoured to."

"Thank you."

The rest of the afternoon was spent catching up with each other on what had been happening in the valley and what Kittal had been discovering in his years away. The women left long before Kittal did and so it was he walked back to the valley alone only to be met by Canaan who had been sent to bring him home. At the sight of his servant Kittal remarked, "just the man."

"Sir?" Canaan cautiously responded.

"Nothing to be alarmed about." He replied as they headed through the valley, homewards, "who was it that injured Deigo?"

After a moment's thought as it had happened three years ago Canaan replied, "it was Joli. Why sir?"

Becoming serious Kittal remarked, "he has got away with it long enough. It doesn't matter how accidental it was, no dragon living in this valley should be harming any man, woman or child that lives here. Where is he to be found? Lead the way Canaan."

"Yes sir."

Joli was nursing his pride from a fight he had fought with another dragon for the right of a female when a stern looking Kittal appeared at his nest, followed by a nervous Canaan. He was a dragon with a blue tint to his scaly skin, odd for the species, the look normally found in the coastal dragons. At some point there had been a coastal dragon in the valley though no one remembered when, not even the dragons. Joli looked puzzled, seeing the way the two men looked. Kittal sat on a rock and said, *"do you remember an incident when you were younger with a young man?"*

Joli's eyes widened and he said uncertainly, *"why?"*

"I am not pleased at the actions that happened. I have seen what you did to Diego." Kittal said seriously.

"I never meant to harm him, I didn't know my own strength." Joli admitted nervously.

"You should have known better than to even touch a young boy with your strength and weight. I know exactly what punishment to give you, but I'll make you suffer until tomorrow morning where I want to see you at the house. What did you think would happen to him?" Kittal said angrily before stalking away not allowing the dragon to answer. The dragon finally found his voice but didn't say anything out of fear of what his punishment might be.

    With the new morning Joli was fearful, he didn't know what was going to happen and he didn't want to know either. He dreaded finding out what Kittal had planned for him. When he had crushed Diego's leg he had been testing himself. He had been turning from child to adult himself. He knew he had done wrong at the time but it had been the first test for him.

    Kittal appeared on the veranda carrying his spare saddle. Diego was hobbling along behind him on his crutches with his father, wondering what was going to happen as much as the dragon. Kittal looked sternly at the dragon. When Diego reached his side he said to Joli, *"this is Diego Joli. As your punishment you'll have to let him ride you like the Suwars. You ruined a young man's life who could one day have saved your life. Having a rider can be an honour and a punishment. For you it is a punishment. You will have to obey Diego until I decide you have done enough."*

Joli bowed his head submissively, *"I understand sir, for how long?"*

"Until one of you die unless I decide differently." Kittal replied sternly, *"now crouch and I'll get this on you."*

    As he got the saddle on the reluctant Joli Kittal said to Diego, "you treat him badly and you'll find yourself in deeper trouble than he is in. I'll teach you how to stay on and use a bow. I need all the fighters I can get which is why I am doing this. Come forward." Kittal beckoned the man towards him and the dragon. Diego cautiously headed over.

From an open window Lulizen watched Kittal and Diego discretely. There was something about the way Kittal was confident with both man and beast that drew her to him. He seemed to be so fatherly to Diego, as if the man was a son he didn't have. Kittal slipped from one tongue to another as he taught both Diego and Joli on what to do as carrier and rider and then turn to Chief Tomas to discuss modifications to the saddle that Diego would need. She was attracted to Diego as well, but she felt it was more out of pity although he was also handsome and closer to her age.

Tania walked over to Lulizen and peered over the other's shoulder asking, "what's happening?"
Lulizen glanced round to see who it was before going back to watching the Dragon and two men working together. She replied, "I'm guessing Diego is going to be riding the Dragon from now on."

"Wow." Tania remarked wide eyed, "that is highly unusual."

"Why?"

"Only father and the Suwars are normally allowed to ride the dragons." Becoming thoughtful Tania went on, "he must be preparing for a fight. We are going to need all the support we can get." Changing the subject she asked, "what do you think of my father?"

Lulizen was growing on her and she wanted to see her father with someone and get the heir she knew he wanted. She knew he had briefly had a mistress from amongst the Suwars before going on his journey and he had been happy then. She wanted him happy again. It would also be nice to feel like a family rather than a group of people randomly thrown together, which even though they were father and daughter, she sometimes felt.

Lulizen looked at Tania wondering what was going through her mind. Feeling embarrassed she smiled before saying, "he's a nice man, he seems to have something about him. I'm surprised that he doesn't have a queue of women wanting him." Lulizen shrugged her shoulders, not really knowing what to say without giving too much away or offending Tania.

Both of them continued to watch Kittal teaching Joli and Diego on how to work together. Both dragon and young man were nervous. Having already crippled the boy Joli feared harming him again and receiving an even worst punishment. While Diego, not wishing to fall off, was shaking so much that he didn't have the balance to remain in the saddle. A part of him also couldn't believe he was being allowed to ride a dragon.

They were so cautious towards each other that it was frustrating Kittal. He forgot that he had grown up with the dragons and been riding them from a young age and Deigo hadn't. After an hour he was too frustrated to go on. He wouldn't normally give up, but he felt like giving up then. To Diego he said, "I'm going to let you two sort it out on your own. I'll continue if you'll just help each other. Diego stop shaking and grip with your knees and get your balance." To Joli he exclaimed, *"Joli stop moving so much. Go do some learning from Kite this afternoon. By the end of the week I want to see you working with Diego as a pair, like naturals."* Turning Kittal threw his hands up in defeat and strode across the lawn, into the house leaving the pair feeling embarrassed.

Both wanted to make Kittal proud of them and they knew they were going to have to work together. Diego slipped off and pulled himself up with a crutch to look Joli in the eye. To the dragon he commented, "how are we going to do this? I can't understand you and you can't understand me."

Joli was thinking a similar thing. He had an idea and pointed at himself with a front claw, *"Joli."*

"I know you are Joli." Diego said in slight annoyance. Joli pointed left and in his language said *"left."*

Catching on Diego repeated what the dragon had said, *"le... f... t."*

The dragon seemed to smile and pointed forward, down, up and right saying the words with Diego repeating them.

Getting excited Diego exclaimed, "we're on to a winner here Joli. Lets go and try. Not to high mind you."

The afternoon drew in and Kittal was surprised to find Diego and Joli still persevering. He shook his head in his disbelief. Watching them they seemed to make a good pair, working together well and he couldn't help being pleased with the results. He slipped away before the pair realised that they were being watched. The next step would be to get Diego using a bow while balancing on the dragon. He decided that he would take them with him on one last flight with Kite.

Eight

No one was expecting visitors a few nights later but the man arrived breathless on a jittery horse which was wide eyed and foaming at the mouth. Hearing the footsteps on the veranda Canaan was sent to find out who it was and take them to the study. Kittal planned to finish dinner first but that wasn't to happen. Canaan ran back in and bent down to murmur in Kittal's ear, "you'd best come sir."
Kittal glanced up into his servant's face and realised something was wrong. He left the women at the table staring as he followed his servant out to the veranda.

The messenger had collapsed into a chair and eagerly accepted the drink Canaan handed to him. His hands were sore and chaffed from holding the reins for most of the day and his hair was soaked with sweat. He tried to stand but Kittal waved it away as he came to stand opposite him and demanded, "what is it?"
Finishing the drink the man looked up, "sir, we were attacked."

"What do you mean attacked? By who?"

"I was sent by the Councillor of Linyee. We were attacked by your brother's men. I was sent as they began so I don't know how many or how much of the town survives."
Kittal turned away and gripped the railing. Damn his brother, he had worked fast. At this time of night there was nothing he could do; not even a dragon could see in the dark. Tonight he would plan and organise and in the morning he would fly over to assess the damage and maybe fly further. He turned

to Canaan, "sort out a bed for him out here and then go and fetch me Chief Tomas,"

"Yes sir." Canaan disappeared.

To the man Kittal said, "there is nothing I can do tonight. My servant is going to make a bed up for you."

The man nodded.

The man woke in the morning as the ground shook as two dragons landed. He stared wide eyed as Kittal appeared dressed to ride carrying his saddle. Behind him came Diego and his father. He watched as the two dragons were saddled and rose into the air with their riders.

Deigo and Joli couldn't believe their luck, that they were flying with their Nejus and Kite. Kite was scowling as she didn't want to be flying with an inexperienced dragon and rider. She enjoyed the flights with Kittal when they were on their own and didn't want to share it. Kittal said to her, *"I don't know what I am going to find so I want to look as strong as possible."*

She grumbled.

He turned and shouted over to Joli, *"no acrobatics. I don't want Deigo to fall off."*

"He won't." Joli answered stubbornly, *"I won't let him."*

Linyee could be seen by the smoke still rising from the smouldering remains of the third of the town that had been burnt. The wall was black there from the fire and smoke. The dragons circled once before landing. The people poured out of the town but hung back at the sight of two dragons. The Councillor pushed his way through the crowd not looking as well manicured as the last time. His hair was dishevelled and there was soot smeared across his forehead. He called out, "Nejus!"

Kittal remained upon Kite, "your messenger arrived last night. I am glad to see that your town is not as badly damaged as I feared."

"We were blessed with a rainstorm sire."

"And who attacked?"

"Men from the town of Whitlani sire. They said they came with Titan's support. We fought back sire. We are loyal to you."

"And I am grateful for that. How many are dead?"

"Five from their party and thirty from Linyee."

"Do you need any assistance?"

"No, but thank you for the offer." The councillor bowed his head.

"I will be on my way then."

"Where do you go sire?" The councillor dared ask.

"To Whitlani."

"Destroy the town for us."

Kittal didn't reply as he was already contemplating it as he said to the dragons, *"let's go."*

They flew east till Whitlani came into view. It was similar to Linyee, but on a lower tell, with fields spreading out around it but unlike Linyee a wooden palisade had been put up around them. There were shouts from the fields and the people in them ran towards the town. They were ready for retaliation but hadn't expected their Nejus and so soon. Men began to appear on the palisade and the town's walls ready to defend themselves.

Above the town Kittal shouted across to Joli, *"stay here. This isn't the time or place for you two to start fighting."* As he turned back he said more quietly to Kite, *"let's go girl. Let's see what this town is made of."*

She smiled as she soared down to the town. Kittal got his bow ready. With a roar she released a stream of fire that licked at the sappy wood and then at the wooden buildings in the town. Kittal fired arrows down at the men but soon found himself having to protect both him and Kite from the arrows being fired at them as one grazed her. The arrow stuck under a scale within reach of Kittal and he pull it out to find it had a long narrow scale piercing head on it. He growled as he knew where that had come from.

As the population turned from defence to saving their town from the growing flames, Kittal nudged Kite away with his knee. Gratefully she turned away as the adrenalin fuelled blood slowed in both of them. They returned to the waiting Joli and Deigo. Showing off she puffed out her chest and boastfully remarked to Joli, *"the work and skill of a Nejus rider and Dragon. What did you think?"*

"Very nice." Joli replied cautiously since he didn't wish to offend the mate of the new Dragon leader, Lupe.

"Better than that I would have thought." Kite remarked back. Before she could say any more Kittal stopped her by saying, *"enough Kite, don't want your ego getting to big otherwise you may do something stupid. Let's go home before anything happens."*

Nine

Six months into Lulizen's training and she had just about mastered the sword but she was struggling with the bow. A tired Kittal put his own bow on the ground to give Lulizen some guidance. He hadn't slept the night before. His dreams had been filled with dragons calling for his help to free them. He wanted to but he needed Kite and his Suwars.

It was an unusually hot sticky day and Kittal suspected that there would be a thunderstorm in a day or two's time. It was so hot that he had stripped off his top to try and stay cool. Sweat was glistening on his naked skin. Lulizen occasionally looked at Kittal wishing it was as easy to remove excess clothing. If she did it would reveal more than she wanted to and so she had to suffer the unbearable heat. She sighed as she took a shot at the butts, not really putting much effort into it so that it fell far too short for Kittal's liking. As he strode over she was glad he hadn't got her practising her sword or staff skills as that would have been unbearable in the heat.

He stood behind her, pressed against her sweaty back. Through her loose sleeved blouse, though currently the excess material was tied up around her shoulders with ties; she could feel his chest rising and falling and his heart beating hard. She smiled to herself as she felt his breath in her ear making her twitch slightly as it tickled.

He was about to take her hand in his and she found herself holding her breath; when Canaan stumbled on to the archery range with an arrow in his shoulder. Canaan fell to his knees as his hand went to the arrow protruding through his shoulder. Lulizen stared as Kittal ran to his servant, "Canaan?"

Through gasps of breath as he tried to fight back the pain, "there…. are a ….. group of….. men in the valley."

"All right. take it easy." He pulled his servant to his feet and took him towards the house. He called out behind, "Lulizen grab my bow and come with us. It's not safe out here."

She hurried ahead to the safety of the house where Tania was on the veranda.

He carried Canaan through to the man's messy bedroom and left him lying on his side. To the two women he said, "stay on your guard and I'll be back as soon as possible." He gave Tania a quick kiss on the cheek and nearly gave Lulizen one but stopped himself as he didn't know how she would react. Tania called out, "be careful yourself father."

With Canaan in his daughter's care he took his bow and quiver from Lulizen. He attached his quiver to his belt where his dragon handled knife hung as he headed out.

The two young women stood at the top of the steps and watched Kittal disappear into the valley. Tania held on to Lulizen unconsciously until the younger managed to prise her fingers off and said, "we should see to Canaan."

Tania turned to go to Canaan while Lulizen stared out for a moment longer as she wished he was still pressed against her back. It had sent shivers through her and she was trying to work out what they had meant. She turned and went in as Tania called for her help.

Kittal made his way to where Canaan first fell and looked round for anywhere an arrow could be fired from. Glancing up he spotted a likely spot and made for it. Up on the rocky protrusion he found the footsteps of several persons and growled to himself, "no one is going to get out alive."

The men moved fast through the grasses and shrubs, thorns catching at their brown clothes of wool and leather. They needed to find a new hiding spot before the real man they should have shot found them. They had been in the valley for two days acclimatising and getting the lay of the land without being discovered by the dragons. Already they were making plans on how to capture the dragons and take them back to Jukirla. They were impressed by the size and health of them.

They paused in a small clearing to catch their breaths and make a decision. They knew they had shot at the wrong man as soon as the man had turned and they had seen the left cheek. The second in command turned to their bearded leader, "what do we do now?"

"We haven't been found yet. We can still take the target down."

"I say we go after a dragon and head home." Another of the group commented.

The other two in the group murmured their agreement.

Kittal crept up on them and silently put an arrow to his bowstring. He caught the end of their discussion and was even more determined to kill them. No one was going to enslave his dragons. He slowly pulled his bow string back and aimed it at one of the group. He needed to split them up so he could take each one down. He released the arrow and it flew into one of the men's heart. The others grabbed their knives and drew closer together as they searched for where the arrow had come from. The leader shouted, "stay close, he can't take us all on."

"Are you an idiot? Did you not hear what he did at the mines?" One of the others protested as he glanced nervously around, "I'm leaving. It's too risky. This is his home territory." The man left the safety of the group but was flung backwards as an arrow entered his chest.

The last three ran but not before another fell with an arrow diagonally through their chest. The last two ran faster with Kittal running behind them through the vegetation. They could hear the rustling and see the movement of the grasses.

Kittal, his bloodlust up, abandoned his bow and quiver and pulled out his knife. He dived through the ten metres of vegetation towards the last two men. They would not be getting out of this valley alive. He leapt from the vegetation, knife in hand. He landed on the bearded leader and yanked his head back by the hair and slit the man's throat. The second in command stumbled, staggered back up and kept running without a glance backwards.

Kittal looked up with a blood splattered face. The hard part was done. It was now one on one and he relished it. He dropped the body he still held by the hair and cleaned his knife on the man's tunic. He stood.

Ahead of him the last man standing found himself up against a rock face with a grass covered ledge above him. He scrabbled up to be able to catch his breath and plan his escape from the valley. He originally wanted to go home and tell them of the fresh dragons to be found and come back armed to the teeth to capture and enslave all of them, but now he wanted to just get out of the valley alive.

As he reached the ledge and climbed over the edge he saw a pair of large eyes watching him in a scaly face. He gulped as the light grey face of the dragon rose up above the nest, glaring at him. He couldn't move, frozen to the spot while the dragon eyed him. She commented, *"you aren't Kittal or Canaan. Who are you?"*
Her tail swung from around her, covered in spines. It swept round the islander and drew him closer so she could see him clearly with her fading eyesight.

Frightened of the spines he moved forward, guided by the tail. As she drew the man towards her she said, *"aren't you going to talk to me? Obviously not. Can you talk at all?"* The man kept his mouth tightly shut although his eyes were wide in fear. He became even more frightened as the dragon sneered, revealing sharp teeth. She remarked, *"no tongue?*

What a pity, I'll just have to kill you then since its obvious you've never seen a Dragon in your life. Have you dear?" She raised a reptile eyebrow in the hope that the man would finally speak to her. With a clawed wing that was minus one sharp claw she reached out and took hold of a leg. It was crushed as she picked him up by the leg, hanging him upside down. The man let out a scream, alerting Kittal to his position. It also gave the dragon a chance to see that he had a tongue. She snarled, *"you lied to me, you have a tongue. I'm not having that."*

Hearing the scream Kittal guessed that a dragon had either disturbed his human prey or vice versa, or it was teasing the man. The only dragon he knew who liked to talk to humans before killing them if they didn't reply or lied was Delia, his own Kite's mother. He ran along the valley floor to where birds had risen into the air in fear at the scream that had come from above them on a ledge in the valley's cliff. Kittal climbed up the rock face and got there in time, as the old slightly senile dragon was about to bite the man's head off. Gasping for breath he said to the dragon, *"stop! Put him down Delia. You should know better. He couldn't answer as he can't understand you."*

The dragon looked angry but put the intruder down. The man crawled across the ledge towards Kittal whimpering in fear. He clung to Kittal's leg, hoping that the man who could speak to the dragon would save him from it. Kittal ignored the man as he spoke to Delia again, *"thank you for stalling him, he is an intruder, but try not to frighten them so much next time."*

"He wouldn't speak and he lied to me, led me to believe he was tongue less." She replied grumpily.

Kittal sighed with a faint smile, *"try not to cause too much trouble for a while since I'm going to need you to take me to Linyee when the festival comes round. Your daughter is nesting and can't do it."*

The elderly dragon seemed to perk up at hearing that Kittal was going to need her. Ever since she had become too old all she could do was hang around moping while Canaan tended to her aching legs. She hadn't had the recognition her daughter had as her own rider, Kittal's father, had never become Nejus. Kittal continued, *"I want you in good health and in a good mood, I'm not having you snapping at the children as I know you have done so in the past."* He eyed her and she looked sheepish for a second before grinning at the memories.

He knocked the valley's intruder out to silent his pleading. Kittal headed down the rock face, one handed, holding the man over his shoulder with his other hand. Delia peered over the ledge looking slightly annoyed that Kittal had stopped her killing the man.

He dropped the man on the wooden floor of the house when he arrived back. Lulizen looked at the intruder with curiosity as she asked nervously, "what did you do to him? Is he dead?"

"Unconscious yes, dead definitely not. Delia had him, broke his leg. Had to knock him out to stop his annoying voice pleading with me. We'll tie him up and wait for him to come round. I want to find some things out before I kill him."

"You can't do that?!" Lulizen protested.

"Why not? He deserves it, causing trouble in this place. You couldn't exactly say he is innocence; he knew what he was doing." Kittal replied sternly, with no emotion in his voice.

"That's unfair, he was only obeying."

"Life isn't fair." Tania said as she came out of Canaan's room, shutting the door behind her. She continued, "If we let him go he'll go back to Titan." To Kittal she said, "I'll get the rope."

"At least one woman obeys. You're going to have to toughen up Lulizen otherwise you won't survive in this place." Kittal said with annoyance to Lulizen making her feel embarrassed. Seeing her blushing cheeks Kittal softened and said to her, "you don't have to watch."

"I'll stay." She replied with determination. She wanted to make Kittal proud of her though she didn't really know why.

It was late evening before their intruder came round to find himself tied to a chair. He struggled to come lose but Kittal's knots were too tight. He called out since there was no one in the room, "hey! What do you want with me?!" Canaan, having recovered enough to be up and about again looked in and saw that the prisoner was awake, fighting the rope. He slipped away to tell Kittal who was dozing on the veranda with Tania and Lulizen. They all went into the prisoner's room. Spotting Kittal the man exclaimed, "you were a crazy man then and you still are."

"That's because you are in my territory now and no one attacks my valley, my dragons or my people and gets away with it." Kittal stood before his prisoner, hands on hips, "why did he send you?"

"I'm not going to say a word." The prisoner glared and spat at Kittal's feet.

For a while Kittal and the man glared at each other. Kittal put the fear of God in the man though the man wouldn't admit it. He remembered what he had heard happened at the mines. Even in a weak state the man had turned out to be vicious in his revenge.

The islander was sweating like a pig, his brown hair sticking to his forehead. He wished he had a drink of water, but he knew he was unlikely to be offered one. The man gulped nervously as Kittal continued to stare at him. Kittal only looked away as Canaan returned to the room with a tray containing a teapot of stewing tea and bowls to drink the tea with.

Most of the room was in darkness so Canaan wandered round lighting the scented oil lamps which would also deter the evening's biting insects humming outside. Kittal waited until Canaan had settled next to Tania and Lulizen on the only other piece of furniture in the room, a low wooden bench with a few cushions on it. Quietly Kittal asked the unnerved man, "I'm guessing that your orders were to kill me?"

The man bit his lip, determined not to say anything. Realising that Kittal already knew the answer to the question he nodded miserably. Kittal commented, "that's one order failed. What about others?"

The man kept his lips sealed. He began to wish that he was back with the dragon who had been planning to kill him quickly. In his view the dragon-speaker was stretching out his death to a painful level.

Thinking of something, almost as if he had read the man's mind, Kittal said, "I could always call for the dragon." He smiled at the man in fake sweetness. The man shook his head viciously, realising he didn't really want to go back to the dragon. Kittal said, "tell me your orders, otherwise I will call for her and she will be glad to do anything I ask to you. You lied to her earlier and she wasn't happy then and is probably not that happy now since I took her new toy away from her. You can have me or her, make up your mind and hurry otherwise you may find it'll be too late for you." Shaking the man said, "you...., don't take me back to that thing." He ended pleading and would have been on his knees if he hadn't been tied up.

"That thing as you so kindly put it does have a name for her species, so kindly remember that." Kittal said sternly, crossing his arms across his chest, "will you talk now? What is Titan planning? What were your orders?" Kittal glared at the man, determined to frighten it all out of him.

The man kept his lips firmly sealed though he had no loyalty to Titan as his paymaster. He just didn't want to die and the longer he said nothing the longer he delayed his death. He thought if he could get through the night he might live. He glanced at the 'audience' and saw that they had fallen asleep unlike Kittal. He sat cross legged on the floor staring at the man. The man was convinced Kittal didn't blink.

Kittal didn't mind waiting, he was ready to wait as long as he needed to. Occasionally he looked over at where

Canaan, Tania and Lulizen had all drifted off. Tania lay against his servant who had an arm round her. He felt that there was more between Tania and Canaan than what met the eye. Whatever it was he didn't mind, for he didn't want Tania to be single all her life and Canaan was a man who he thought was suitable for his daughter.

He was attracted to Lulizen. Trying to work out how she felt towards him frustrated him more and more these days. His thoughts wandered more and more to having an heir from their mixed blood. It was like she was leading him on half the time and the other half confusing him. He hadn't felt like that in a long time, not since Tania's mother.

He turned his gaze back to their captive to wait patiently for the man to speak. The man closed his eyes to try and block out Kittal's eyes. He knew he wasn't going to be able to remain silent forever but was willing to have a good try at doing so. He opened his eyes to see Kittal still watching him with an intent look. Seeing it he got annoyed and blurted out, "I don't know his plans. We were given our orders and brought here to do them."

At his cry the three on the cushioned bench jumped and stared round trying to remember where they were. Kittal smiled at his prisoner, "and your orders were?"

"Kill you. Capture the woman." The man nodded his head towards Tania who stared in disbelief. She asked, pointing at herself, "me?"

Wanting to protect her Canaan hugged her closer to him while she looked on frightened. She turned to look at her father for answers. To her he said, "I won't let Titan lay even a finger on a hair of your head." Turning to their prisoner he asked, "once you had her what were you supposed to do?"

"Take her back to him, don't ask me what he wants her for." He said playing ignorance.

Thoughtfully Kittal eyed the man. He had a feeling the man knew more than what he was saying. The man seemed to know that Kittal knew he wasn't saying everything and gulped nervously. He had already said more than he should have and sealed his lips.

Another hour went by and Kittal was growing impatient. He stood to stretch his legs and began walking round the room. He ran a hand over a rack of swords, pausing long enough for the prisoner to gulp nervously. From across the room Kittal asked, "want to talk?"

The man shook his head.

Kittal walked over from behind. He reached round and grabbed the man's right hand, startling the prisoner. He pressed the hand against the arm of the chair and snapped the smallest finger backwards, breaking it. The prisoner screamed. Lulizen stared in shock.

After several of his fingers had been broken tears were running down his face from the excruciating pain. His breath came out in whimpers. Kittal walked round and crouched down, "ready to talk?"

"Just no more." He moaned.

"What are his plans then?" Kittal demanded.

"Become Nejus, assuming we had killed you. He knows that you have no heir yet." The man guessed, just to give his torturer an answer.

"And?"

"We get the dragons."

Tania stood and hissed, "he'll just have to do it the hard way. My father is not going to let him win." She ran from the room followed by Canaan. Kittal looked thoughtful. His daughter was tough but then this seemed to have affected her. Lulizen sat, immobile, on the bench looking stunned.

Kittal crossed the room and took a sword from the rack. He looked stern as he pulled the blade from its scabbard. The orange beginnings of dawn reflected on the blade. He approached the Jukirlan and quietly said, "prepare to meet your Gods. You were a brave man to last so long, but you deserve a better life now." He bowed to the man in respect, "hold your head up high, you should be proud of yourself to last under my torture."

Trembling all over the man held up his head so the slice would be a clean one. Kittal asked, "do you wish to know whether death has a face or not?"

The man tried to answer but found no words were coming out of his mouth. He shut it in his embarrassment and Kittal quietly commented, "there is no need to be ashamed, no one willingly goes to their next life. I have been close to going there myself and have no wish to go there just yet. To live on I promised not to tell so don't ask me what it is like." He gave the man a small smile as he moved round to the man's side. The man returned the smile as his head dropped from his body. Kittal had sliced through his neck in one go since his blade was sharp enough to go straight through bone.

Diego didn't know what to say when Kittal gave him a round parcel as he sat in his saddle on Joli. Kittal said to the young man, "I want you to drop it over Titan's castle. Don't try to do anything foolish. Drop it off and come straight back, you are more useful alive than dead." He stepped away from the Dragon and rider and waved them off as they rose into the air to head towards Titan's castle. To himself Kittal said, "that boy will go a long way if he keeps his head on straight." He headed back into the house in the hope of getting some undisturbed sleep. He flopped on to his bed, stretching out to try and stay as cool as possible in the calm before the storm.

Ten

It was several more days before the storm decided to break. It became so hot and humid Kittal was thinking about making an offering to the Brothers of the Sky for the weather to break.

As a new day dawned he felt the weather was going to break and it would start raining. The skies which had been clear were beginning to cloud over with darkening clouds as the Brothers prepared for a grand finale in the month's weather.

No one was willing to do anything and just lay around trying to cope with the tedious sticky heat. They took it in turns to fetch large jugs of water, reluctantly peeling themselves from their seats. They all hung around Kittal's bedroom, which was the coolest room of the house with the smallest of breezes barely going through.

Kittal was lying on the floor of his room where it was coolest, his eyes half closed. With a sigh he slowly stood and walked out, restless. The others glanced up but didn't react from where they lay sprawled out in the sitting room. He wandered barefoot from the house to nowhere in particular. He found himself drawn to Delia's nest.

She was surprised to see him as he appeared on her ledge. She said, *"what a surprise. Two visits in a matter of days. What brings you here Nejus?"*
He sat down next to the old dragon, leaning against her soft belly. He sighed and closed his eyes, trying to find the courage to ask the elderly dragon for advice. She looked at

him, waiting patiently while she was in a good mood. He finally spoke, *"what would you do if you knew that you had found the prefect mate, but she didn't seem to be very interested in you?"*

"Are you just trying to replace Her?" She asked.

"She'll always be there, but I need an heir. I'm not going to live forever."

"You could if you wanted to." Delia pointed out. Questioning him again she asked, *"is this more for practicality than love?"*

"I feel something for Lulizen, it has yet to reach love, but given time, maybe." He shrugged his shoulders, *"I've waited so long I don't want to appear desperate."*

"You'll just have to be patient Kittal. You must wait for her to come to you."

"What if she feels the same but doesn't want to tell me from embarrassment? I don't want to remain single for the rest of my life. I enjoyed being married and having a young child."

"If you can't wait you'll have to encourage her to reveal her feelings. Tell her what you feel and see how she reacts." Delia returned knowledgeably, *"one must speak out for the other to respond and now isn't a particularly bad time to find out."* She shifted her position making Kittal stand up. He looked at her thoughtfully and before he climbed down he commented, *"if everything goes wrong I'll blame it on you."*

"No problem Nejus." She called out as Kittal's head vanished below her ledge. With him gone she settled to sleep since the heat was making her drowsy.

Back at the house Canaan reluctantly rose to do his chores. He had put them off for as long as possible. Tania gazed after him with a small smile. Lulizen rolled over and caught the look and said, "why don't you tell your father that you want to be with Canaan?"

Tania sat up and hugged her knees, "do you know what it's like?"

"What is what like?" Lulizen asked, looking puzzled.

"Sleeping with a man."

Lulizen laughed but realising she had embarrassed Tania she stopped. It was obvious that the young woman was almost completely innocence on the matter having no mother, sisters or other women around to discuss it or overhear about sex. She said, "I'm guessing you've never done it?"

"Not all the way. We just…" Tania shifted uncomfortably, "… you know."

Two years back she had found a book in her father's library with lots of sexual positions. She and Canaan had worked their way through it doing everything but the final deed, full penetration.

"I've not even done that. I just know bits from what my maids have said to each other."

"Oh, sorry. I don't know why I thought you knew more." Tania remarked.

Out of curiosity Lulizen asked, "how do you know that you love Canaan?"

"How did you guess? Do you think my father knows?"

"I… I don't know. Maybe because I am a woman and a romantic. I wouldn't know if your father knows." Lulizen answered feeling uncomfortable under Tania's studious stare. There was a part of her that was wary of Kittal now having seen how he could be a cold-blooded killer but coming from a ruling family she knew it was important to protect country and family by any means necessary. Apart from that she couldn't stop feeling something for Kittal which she wasn't sure what it was.

"I believe you. It's true, I do love Canaan. He makes me so happy and warm and wanted. It started when father was away travelling. There were only the two of us." Tania admitted shyly, not catching Lulizen's eye. Moving the conversation away from herself Tania asked, "what about you and father?"

"What do you mean?"

"Well, you wouldn't ask me how I know that I love Canaan otherwise. Come on, he's not here to hear."

Lulizen blushed, "I am…."

"Am what?" Tania moved closer to Lulizen.

"I do like Kittal, a lot." Lulizen sat up.

"A lot?"

"I don't love him."

"But you could?"

"Maybe." Lulizen wouldn't make eye contact with Tania. She felt tingles when close to Kittal and wanted to feel his hands on her and his naked body pressed to hers like the day when Canaan was injured. However, she wasn't sure if it was all sexual attraction or attraction for the whole man.

"What are you going to do?" Tania interrupted Lulizen's thoughts.

"I don't know. Don't tell him." Lulizen hurriedly ended with fear. She didn't want to embarrass either herself or Kittal with her emotions. If it came out and Kittal wasn't interested she would be mortified and felt she would have to leave the valley she had come to love.

Tania moved closer to Lulizen and put her arms round her. Over the time spent in the valley she had begun to think of Lulizen as a friend and the sister she had never had. Tania murmured, "I promise not to say anything. One day soon I'm sure we'll both get what we want." She ended with a sigh and stared out through the open doorway, hoping to see Canaan come past and maybe smile at her.

"Hopefully." Lulizen replied quietly.

They fell silent as both thought about men, sex and love. Lulizen was the one to disturb the silence. She said to Tania, "I think you should go ahead and do it if that is what both of you want. There's nothing stopping you from doing it if you both love each other. Kittal hasn't exactly told you that you can't, so take the chance."

"You think so?" Tania's eyes widened at Lulizen telling her to have sex.

"Yes." Lulizen answered firmly with a wishful smile, "then let me know what it's like."

The young women giggled together but fell silent to save themselves from embarrassment when Canaan appeared. He gave Tania a loving but slightly suspicious look making Lulizen smile at seeing the pair's obvious love for each other. She wouldn't admit it, but she felt a little jealous observing Canaan lightly touching Tania's shoulder and she touching his fingers with hers. She hadn't been interested in men, love and sex before meeting Kittal probably because she had been something for men to be in awe of back in the mountains.

They all headed to bed early, Tania and Canaan planning more than just sleeping. Lulizen lay on top of her bed in her thin nightdress, made by Tania, thinking over her discussion with Tania. She couldn't see that she would love Kittal, but maybe in the future. She wondered if she should tell Kittal or not and then there was the sex issue. Since the conversation with Tania she now wanted to know what it was like for herself. She contemplated what she should do and wondered if Kittal might be awake. Making a decision she rolled off her bed and slipped through the house to Kittal's bedroom where an oil lamp was turned down low.

She found him asleep and felt slightly let down. He lay on his right side sleeping peacefully. With a soft smile Lulizen crept across the room and on to his bed. Only as she got to the bed did she notice that he was completely naked. Was he expecting her to appear tonight? But it was a hot night as the storm still hadn't arrived and he might always sleep naked.

He stirred but didn't roll over so she guessed he didn't know she was planning to come, not that she had known until minutes ago herself. She smiled as she lay on her side and drew the back of her finger down the length of scar on his face. He sighed in his sleep and seemed to smile for a microsecond. Lulizen had to stifle a giggle as she allowed her fingers to draw themselves down Kittal's arm.

Feeling the soft touch on his arm Kittal rolled over, quietly moaning with the beginnings of a smile curling up the corners of his mouth. Lulizen whispered, "Kittal."

He opened his eyes slowly and looked up at Lulizen who was smiling down at him. He reached up with a hand and guided her head down. He placed a kiss on her lips, which she returned willingly. She lay on top of him, kissing him. His hands began to pull up her nightdress.

She slipped out of it as they rolled over so Kittal came out on top. He began to kiss her throat as she held on to his arms. He began to move down. Her body was quivering with sexual nervousness leaving her gasping from the pleasure of it all. He smiled as he returned to her lips and murmured, "there is no need to be afraid. I will be gentle." He felt his blood rushing round his body from the touch of her skin against his. He hadn't been with a woman for a long time and to have a young lithe body in his hands was exciting.

Softly he moved down Lulizen's body. He squeezed her plump breasts, feeling her nipples harden under his fingers' touch. He kissed them as he slipped a hand between her thighs. She clenched and then tentatively relaxed as she began to feel sensations she had never thought she would feel. He wouldn't be stopping too soon unlike when she had explored herself.

She could feel his large erection pressing her stomach and was not sure what to make of it. His fingers stroked her and she felt herself becoming aroused and began to react back to his knowledgeable touches. She began to arch her back and her breath became ragged as the pleasures she was feeling mounted up inside her body.

He pulled her up on to his thighs and she found herself biting her lip. He raised an eyebrow in question. She gave a nod of permission and closed her eyes and held her breath as he entered her. As if anticipating this moment there was a crash of thunder and flash of lightening as the storm finally broke over their heads. She grabbed hold of him, clinging to him through the short, tight moment of pain, as he took her virginity. Moments later the rain began to fall in torrents, rattling on the tiles.

Slowly they broke apart, breathing heavily, wrapped in the bed sheets. He lay back on his pillows and opened his mouth to say something but thought better of it. He glanced at Lulizen, "are you alright?"

She cautiously nodded. She was a little stunned at herself. Had she really initiated the sex? She didn't feel guilty about doing it as in her parents' eyes she was married and in the valley she was free to do what she wanted. She listened to the rain as she drifted off to sleep. Kittal turned his head to look at Lulizen, her black hair framing her head on the pillow next to him and couldn't help smiling.

The rain continued on through the night and well into the morning. Neither couple cared since they didn't want to leave their beds to get up and do the few daily chores that needed to be done. Kittal lay with his arms wrapped round Lulizen, his head peering over her shoulder. He nibbled her ear making her giggle. She asked, "what if Tania or Canaan come in?"

"They don't matter." He mumbled and kissed her neck. She relaxed, allowing him to do what he wanted as they slipped under the sheet. Under the sheet Kittal murmured, "I care for you so much, I wouldn't be able to live without you if you left."

"What about your deceased wife?"

Kittal stopped what he was doing and stared down at her with a concerned look, "she'll always be in my heart, but I care deeply for you as well. I must move on and you are the one." He gave her a long kiss on the lips to silence any more questions she may have had.

When they finally did get up all of them were looking bright eyed from what they had been up to during the night. Canaan had a bounce in his step as he went about his work. Kittal looked at Tania with a knowing smile, which she returned sheepishly. When they had a private moment together he said to her, "it's all right Tania, I never wanted you to be untouchable for the rest of your life. You deserve Canaan he is a good man."

Tania smiled with relief and hugged her father tightly, "thank you. Thank you for being so understanding."

"Of course I can be. I will have a word with Canaan as I don't want him to hurt you." He gave his daughter's arm a gentle squeeze of reassurance before wandering away. He felt pleased for his daughter that she hadn't been totally alone in his absence and that she had found someone who made her happy, even if it was his manservant. He wondered whether Lulizen made him happy or whether the night had just been sexual release for both of them.

    The rain stopped late in the afternoon whereupon Kittal took the chance to take Lulizen out into the valley. He led her deep into the dripping and steaming green vegetation that now shone bright in the sun. She wondered what he was up to as holding her hand he guided her up the side of the valley on a narrow path of foot eroded steps. She quickly lost count of the steps but felt sure there must have been at least eight hundred. Reaching the top he told her to close her eyes. He led her blindly forward and then stopped and turned her to face in one direction. In her ear he whispered, "open your eyes."

    She opened them slowly, frightened that she wouldn't like what she was going to see. She was speechless for a moment as she gazed out across the valley that was stretching out in front of her. In the centre of her sight was the house surrounded by its green lawn with the dirt arena off to one side. Near to the arena was a brown clearing she didn't know anything about, the camp site for the Suwars when they were in the valley. The other side of the valley reared up on the far side, grey against the greenery.

    "It's amazing." She mumbled, turning to look at Kittal, who she had expected to find still behind her but he wasn't there.

    He had wandered off to what appeared to be a partially ruined temple. Lulizen scrambled after him, not wanting to be so close to the edge without him nearby to save her if she fell. The temple consisted of many arches, most of them complete. Twisted round the support columns were dragons as if they were climbing up to the arches. Hanging down from the complete arches were banners of silk soaked at the moment from the rain though they normally danced in a breeze. To one side was an altar and behind that was a statue of a Dragon. It was half the size of a real one but it still looked immense in stature.

Kittal was knelt down in front of the altar, his forehead touching the stone floor. He stood after touching the floor another three times and smiled softly at Lulizen as he asked, "what do you think of this place?"

"It's incredible, but what is this place?"

"The ancient Temple of the Dragons. My forefathers used to be the high priests of this place, worshipping the five main Dragon tribes. The dragons decided they no longer wanted to be worshipped and asked to be protected and looked after instead, wishing no longer to be thought of as Gods. They gave my family the ability to speak the dragon tongue so we could do everything right. Since then this place has only been used for certain ceremonies like the joining of the Nejus with his mate and the enrolling of a new Nejus." Kittal explained to Lulizen, "I know it is so soon but now I know how you feel it is my turn to show you how I feel. I brought you up here in the hope you'll become my wife."

"I... I...." Lulizen said as she stumbled over her words in her surprise.

"You may think it over if you wish."

"You have caught me by surprise." She couldn't think straight.

She turned away so as not to see Kittal's hopeful face. Thinking about it, maybe her father had seen something in Kittal at their meeting which meant he knew his daughter would be safe with the dragons' Lord Defender. She wondered if she should trust her father's instincts. One thing she did know was that she didn't want to leave such a beautiful valley and the close honest relationships she had formed, especially with Tania. She pursed her lips in serious contemplation. Should she? Should she not? A decision made she turned back to Kittal, "I will happily become your wife." Kittal beamed, relieved that she had accepted his offer. He took one of her hands and remarked, "everything will be just fine, don't you worry. When the Suwars come we will be joined, but until then you will be my wife whatever others may say."

"Suwars?"

"You will find out about them later, there are other things of more importance for the moment like the Dragon Festival. You will accompany me there as the Lady of Dragons I hope."

Eleven

The first day of the Dragon Festival was spent with the villagers of the valley joining the Nejus' family on the lawn of the house. It had begun with Kittal appearing at the top of the steps in his red ceremonial robes over a grey sleeveless tunic embroidered with silver thread. (Lulizen, over time, had come to realise these were his colours of choice after having found the storeroom of old armour, weapons and colours.) His hair had been washed and glimmered in the sunlight. Around his neck he wore a large medallion.

He held up a hand and the villagers, dressed in their best, grew silent. To them he said, "I am glad to be alive to see another Dragon Festival. And this year I wish to present to you my soon to be wife and new Nejusana." He turned and a beaming Tania pushed a slipper footed blushing Lulizen out of the house.

She wore a dress with a skirt of flowing layered silk of red and gold. It had square neckline and cinched in at the waist. Over the top of it she wore a heavier cloth in red like Kittal's, which formed a coat embroidered with a female dragon, hovering over an egg, in sliver thread. She wore a veil over her long soft black plaited hair and round her throat were a double row of pearls from the box of jewellery Kittal had presented to her.

He took her hand while smiling at her. The villagers cheered and clapped. Now there was a chance of an heir for their Nejus so they didn't have to worry that Titan would one day replace him. They knew Kittal would now fight even harder for his lands.

Lulizen glanced behind as she felt Tania step behind her also dressed like her in a light grey dress with a red coat over the top. With Tania now present as well Kittal led them and the villagers up to the Temple of the Dragons. The arches had been hung with new banners and garlands of flowers. Crouched around the temple were the dragons including the two newly hatched mountain ones.

In rows the humans bowed to the dressed altar. A bowl of flames flickered on the stone altar. Another bowl sat waiting for Kittal's offering with a knife before it. Canaan appeared from behind an arch and lit several sticks of incense which he then carried along the rows. Kittal rolled up a sleeve and picked up the knife. He cut across his wrist and allowed the blood to drop into the bowl, mixing with the herbs within it. As blood ran down his arm he raised the bowl to the sky, "Oh Great One bless your children for another year. Bless those enslaved with the strength to go on. Bless those recently born to grow up strong and wise. Look after those who have joined you in the heavens."

He poured the mix into the bowl of embers which hissed and spat before the flames rose higher and brighter. They turned green to blue to purple to red before disappearing. Kittal bowed before the altar and the villagers followed suit as a horn was blown.

With the solemnity of the ceremony done with the feasting and dancing began. The tables were laid, and a pig roasted along with plenty of chickens over a fire pit. The children ran round the lawn chasing the peacocks. The young women shyly approached a bemused Lulizen for her blessings while their partners received one from Kittal where they sat, relaxed, on the steps of the veranda as the sunset behind the house.

Formalities were over now that the feast had come to an end and the music started for dancing. Village dogs shared the remains of the feast with those picking at the bones. He smiled at her, "I would like to think we need theirs as well for a happy and success joining."

The couple standing before them laughed and then reached for each other's hands. They bowed to their Lord before running off into the vegetation.

"I think we should do the same." Kittal winked at Lulizen making her blush, "run off and have sex like young lovers."

"I think we'd best stay here." Lulizen said trying to look serious though she liked the idea.

He leant over and kissed her as Canaan brought them glasses of wine.

The second day had another early start as they prepared to go to Linyee. As she dressed Lulizen for a second time Tania fought to hide her jealousy. She had always enjoyed attending Linyee's Dragon Festival celebrations with her father and in his place in his absence. And now it would be Lulizen going. She pulled the sash just a little too tight causing Lulizen to gasp in protest; but then she remembered she would get to spend the day with Canaan. That morning he had whispered to her all he planned to do to her and with her, inspired by the book. She smiled to herself.

She and Canaan watched from the veranda as Kittal and Lulizen crossed the lawn to the saddled Delia. Kittal helped Lulizen on to Delia's back as he said to the dragon, *"take it easy will you, I can handle your flying style, but she may not be able to do so."*

"I'll try my best Nejus."

"On your best behaviour remember." He remarked sternly.

"I never planned to be on anything else." The dragon replied stubbornly, *"don't bother me with such things."*

"Who is in charge here?" Kittal asked, eyeing the old dragon. The dragon ignored the question and huffed, turning away from looking at the man. Kittal poked the dragon in the side and demanded, *"answer my question."*

"You are in charge sir." Came the sulky reply.

"Thank you, don't sulk." He said as he climbed into his saddle on the dragon's back.

The dragon rose into the air at his command frightening Lulizen so much she clung to the arm Kittal had round her. Behind her he smiled and said loudly to Delia, *"take it easy. I'm not the only one up here."* The dragon slowed her pace, her wings beating up and down as they flew along over the green land of the savannah.

They soon arrived at Linyee where coloured banners were out, whipping in the plain's wind. Everyone was dressed in their best and brightest clothes for the celebrations. Food and drinks stalls along with market stalls were set up waiting for the money to begin flowing. This year they had even more to celebrate as their Nejus was back and had defended the honour of the town by attacking their unlikely enemy. They eagerly watched as Delia came to a clumsy stop on the edge of town.

As Kittal helped Lulizen down she clutched at her stomach. She had felt a little queasy all morning and for the last few days and the flight had made her feel worst. He asked with concern, "are you well?"

She gave him a tight smile as the town's councillor walked forward, "I'll be all right. I think it was the flying."

They both turned to the Counciller as he bowed to Kittal, "welcome to Linyee on this fine day my Lord, an ideal one for celebrating the Dragon Festival."

"Yes, it is, quite." Kittal replied stiffly, he wasn't a man for pleasantries when it came to official situations.

"Would your lady care for a drink and some shade?" The councillor asked as he glanced at Lulizen, wondering where she had come from. Kittal turned and looked at her questioningly. Lulizen smiled as she replied, "please."

"If you'll both come this way." The councillor led the way through the gathering people who stepped back out of the way in respect for their Lord. He continued, "We are glad to have you back in the celebrations. The past years have not been as good as they should have been." He smiled kindly as he directed them to the best pair of chairs under the protection of an awning. Kittal didn't say anything at the comment. He settled himself in the chair and took a goblet offered to him. Lulizen thanked the woman who brought her a similar one with a shy smile.

She felt a bit like she was back at court except that she was exposed to all instead of hidden behind a screen. There had been ceremonies and festivals back at home as the maids were quite often allowed time off to go and enjoy them in the town below the court where everyone lived and supplied the palace. They would come back giggling and whispering about mischievous masked figures trying to look under their skirts and magicians and dancers and the food stalls while she, Lulizen, had been stuck with her female relatives playing cards or reading or staring blankly into space rather than sew.

With their Lord now there, the celebrations began in earnest. From the main gate of the walled town at the bottom of the rocky outcrop, came a bearded snake like dragon, which swayed as it drew closer to the crowds. From behind the crowds the real dragon eyed it suspiciously, ready to burn it with fire if it threatened Kittal in anyway. Thankfully for the townsfolk she didn't do anything. There would have been in a real panic if the real dragon had let lose its fiery breath on the dancers inside the paper dragon and some just about remembered a time when Delia had done just that as a young dragon.

Another dancing dragon joined the first and then a third appeared. All three began to entwine with each other in an elaborate dance, which had been handed down to each new generation. Suddenly they swung away from each other and twisted round to head straight for Kittal. Lulizen felt nervous, fearing they were going to do something to her and Kittal. They stopped a few feet away. She breathed a sigh of relief as the three dragons bowed their bearded heads towards

Kittal and her. The heads came off and the men inside bowed to Kittal as he looked at them.

There was a nervous silence as everyone waited for their Lord's reaction. He looked intently at the three man who had been the heads for a moment before saying, "I have never thought I would miss that dance, but seeing it made me realise that I have. It was superbly done, well done." He stood and rested a hand on each of the young men's shoulders blessing each one. They looked wide-eyed at Kittal surprised that they had been blessed. Kittal smiled at them as he remarked, "there is no need to look so frightened. This is a day to be enjoyed. I don't know about you but I am enjoying it so far. Let's hope it only gets better."

A cheer went up from the crowd as his spoken words were passed through the people. As he sat down again a band of musicians appeared who formed an alley for the troop of dancers in colourful flowing dresses to come down. They spun round the circle formed by the happy townspeople. They floated away into the crowd, but the music continued to play though the dancers had vanished from view. People took it as a cue to begin dancing. Gradually couples filtered out of the gathered people to dance to the music, joining the children who were already jumping up around giggling in the dance space.

With the formal part over with the crowd began to spread out to dance, eat and drink, and watch the other entertainments and buy the nomads' wares. Older folk found shade under the set-up awnings where they chattered and looked after the little ones if asked to.

Lulizen wondered if she and Kittal were to remain seated, but he got up. He offered her a hand with a bow and once she had taken it, he led her on to the ground in front of the musicians. Smiling at her he began to dance, holding her close. He led her in the steps since she didn't really know what she was supposed to be doing, stumbling over his feet occasionally. He didn't complain as she soon sorted out her footsteps, following him, allowing him to lead with good grace. She closed her eyes, trusting him to guide her everywhere.

She didn't hear the music stop and silence fall. She only noticed as Kittal kissed her. She opened them slowly, surprised by what he had done in public. She smiled shyly as the people of Linyee clapped energetically. She blushed and stared at her feet. Kittal laughed good-humouredly at her as he led her back under the awning. He said quietly, "you were beautiful out there, any children will be like you."

"How do you know?" She asked.

"I don't, I'm making it all up. You were terrible out there, walking all over my feet. I'll have to take you back." He smiled cheekily and winked at her. She glared at him for a moment and muttered, "beast."

"I'll take that as a compliment then." He said brightly. She looked him in his eyes and saw only good humour in them, his laughter lines emphasising the humour. She hadn't seen him so happy, not even when she had accepted his proposal. He was enjoying showing her off.

The celebrating continued late into the evening with scented torches being lit as the night began to fall. They took part in many dances as a couple. The drinks and snacks kept coming. She grew tired as it had been a long day and turned to Kittal to tell him so, "is it not time to leave?"

"Not yet. There are the fireworks to watch first. Now, I believe this is the last dance." He stood and held out a hand, "shall we?"

Reluctantly she took it and they stepped down from the dais. The other dancers stopped and stepped away to watch as Kittal and Lulizen slowly turned in a small circle. Lulizen rested her head against his chest with a faint smile. He murmured, "tonight will be the best you will ever have had and that's a promise."

"What if I say no?"

"You won't." He smiled as he opened his eyes to stare out across the audience. The music came to an end but the pair continued to turn slowly.

The rockets began to leap into the sky and bursting into a rain of multi-coloured sparks. Children covered their ears against the loud noise of exploding gunpowder. More rockets screamed into the air, twisting as they did and ending in a crackling fall of sparks. Candles spat into life to create a fountain of colour, changing colour until their energy was spent.

As suddenly as it had begun silence fell on the quiet townspeople. They continued to stare up at the sky remembering all of the fireworks as the smoke produced floated away on the breeze. As they began to talk they realised that it had grown cold since the early evening. They pulled their clothes tighter around them and began to slowly wander back into the town. The nomads began to pack up their stalls. Kittal led the way over to Delia, an arm round Lulizen and the town's councillor following behind. Kittal turned to the councillor and said, "thank you, it was very enjoyable and pleasant. Let's hope we are all still around to see it next year."

"I certainly agree with that my Lord." The councillor bowed low though he hadn't quite understood Kittal's last sentence, "may you have a safe journey home."

"I will." Kittal smiled faintly. The councillor stepped back to watch his Lord help Lulizen on to the dragon's back and then climb on himself. The dragon stretched its wings to their full length before rising into the air, leaning into a turn to face the right direction of home and the valley.

Flying back by the light of the full moon Lulizen glanced up at the stars, wondering if they were called by the same names as her people. Looking for the three most recognisable stars in a triangle, twinkling bright in the night sky, she asked, "Kittal, you see those three stars close together? What do you call that group?"

Kittal turned to look and replied, "that group are the three sisters. Each of those stars is a dragon long since deceased. Up there somewhere will be Old Narl and one day Delia will join him, nearby. The three sisters were born out of the same egg which is a very rare event."

"What about people like you?"

"We don't go up there to be remembered. We are not as important as the dragons. They were here long before us and have influenced the way the people live in so many ways." She leant backwards, into his chest as he put an arm round her protectively. She sighed thoughtfully, "they are beautiful though, don't you think?"

"Mmmm." Kittal replied vaguely, "very." He stared straight ahead with a thoughtful expression on his face.

"What are you thinking about?"

"Nothing." He probably replied too quickly but Lulizen didn't notice. Her questions had risen in him a reminder of his mortality and that as yet he had no heir. He wondered if Lulizen was pregnant yet.

"Kittal, can I ask you something?"

"Of course you can."

"Are my people descended from yours?"

"Aah." Kittal smiled, "I am one step ahead of you. I was using your father's library to find out what had occurred to the Suwars who had abandoned the valley many years ago. They disagreed with one of my ancestors. And also the last mountain dragon gave me some of the information I needed."

"And?"

"Yes, they are your ancestors and I feel your blood harks back to them."

She smiled to herself, liking the idea of having the blood of Suwars within her, no matter how diluted.

Twelve

Waking in the morning Kittal just wanted to go back to sleep. He tried to turn over but Lulizen was pressed up tight against him. He smiled and closed his eyes, preparing to sleep again though he was more likely to toss and turn.

Lulizen was forced to wake up when she heard a cry of fear come from Kittal. She sat up and looked at the man by her side. His face was twisted up with emotion as it turned, his mouth saying unuttered words. Cautiously Lulizen touched him and his eyes sprung open. He stared round feeling terrified still. He looked at his hands. His nightmare had taken him back to the mines of Jukirla where he had gained bloody and raw hands and where he had killed many men with them. He was relieved to see them healed and tanned with no broken and cracked nails.

Lulizen looked down at him with concern and he became worried, "what was I doing?"

"It was a nightmare, that is all."

"I must rescue them."

"Rescue who?"

He sat up, "I must contact my sister. I need the Suwars. I hoped they would have been here by now." He pushed himself off the bed and wandered round the room gathering clothes.

She watched him from the bed, smiling quietly, loving every ounce of him and his scarred body and the fact she had a feeling she was carrying his child as her monthly bleeding had not come. The thought took her by surprise and as if he felt the surprise he turned and looked at her with a raised eyebrow. She shyly nodded. He strode over to her and kissed her hard on the lips and murmured, "I am glad."

He returned to getting dressed and kissed Lulizen again before picking up his bracelet from the desk. He reassured her, "I'll be back. I will be a while but it will be long before the day ends."

"Take care."

Kittal leant on the bed and said, "with them here we will get joined, what we have been waiting for." He smiled at her. There was a moment's hesitation on Lulizen's part before she gave him a kiss. With her own smile she pushed him off the bed saying, "go do what you need to do and then you'll be back a lot sooner."

He strolled through the valley to the ruined temple. He filled a large shallow dish with water in a hidden corner of the temple. He held the bracelet cupped in his hands and concentrated on it. Slowly it began to glow red and spin and then he placed it in the still water of the dish. He knelt before the dish as the ripples disappeared and a young face appeared looking similar to his sister but was not her. He frowned, "where is Ciara?"

"I am her daughter Leanne."

"You have grown. Fetch her please." He softened.

After a moment Ciara's face appeared. She smiled warmly at her older brother as she pushed golden brown hair out of her blue eyes, "it has been a long time Kittal."

"It has but now I have returned."

"What do you want?"

"The return of my Suwars. I was surprised you didn't come for the Festival. I am in need of them to rescue dragons and also remind Titan he is not ruler of Keytel."

"He proposed a joint rule while you were gone." Ciara remarked with a frown, "rescue dragons?"

"I'll explain more when you arrive."

"There is more?" Ciara remarked, eyeing her brother's image in her own dish.

"You miss nothing sister. I have something special to tell you. I have found myself a new mate and we are only waiting for the presence of you and your Suwars to be joined." He smiled.

"Does she know what she's getting into?"

"She has learnt to use the sword and bow already."

"I meant more on the ceremony Kittal. I know you would prepare her for life in this land of ours, but you always forget about ceremonies, which everyone else always worries about, except maybe you."

"I was hoping you would go through it with her. You are better than I will ever be at explaining things like that."

"Coward." Ciara said, but she couldn't help smiling to herself. She had just proved yet again that she knew her brother far too well, too well for his or her own good sometimes, "I'll go through it with her, don't worry, just you be careful with her on the day."

"I will, you have my word." Kittal promised.

"Tell me about her then." Ciara asked.

"She is from the mountains and I have found out interesting things about her people. She is a caring woman and feisty. There is a sense of power in her from her ancestors. She is the best woman I have met since Her death."

"Who are her ancestors?"

"Our own. Some of us left this land to tame a tribe of wild mountain dragons. I found their history buried in the pile of scrolls I have and to think we thought the tale was a legend."

"Oooh." Ciara sounded intrigued and then added, "I will see you in three days time and I look forward to seeing you again and meeting her." She dipped a hand in her bowl.

Kittal sat back with a smile. It was good to see that Ciara was well after three and a half years though he sensed sadness in her.

He reached for the bracelet but found the water boiling and spitting. He tried to get the bracelet out but the water was too hot. Without warning the water erupted upwards and the bracelet shattered in the dish. He moaned and pressed his hands to his head as he felt all the power contained in it swirl around him before being absorbed into his body. It had survived the last four years only to break apart now. He fainted.

Coming round he carefully sat up and looked down at his hands. They glowed with the magic in him. He groaned, he was going to have to make another bracelet before all the powerful magic now flowing through him killed him. It was magic bestowed upon the Nejus many hundreds of years ago by the Dragon Lord until the first realised that a man's body could not cope with its strength. Ever since Nejuses had made a vessel to contain most of the magic. It had been contained in different forms over the years. He had chosen a bracelet form as it was easier to carry with him either on his wrist or in a bag and it was discreet for when he had travelled incognito.

He stumbled to his feet and swayed. Carefully he took a step and as he didn't drop to his knees he headed down the steps and back to the house.

Lulizen was there to welcome him but he snapped at her smiling face, "don't touch me as I could easily kill you." Her happy face fell away and she looked frightened, what was going on?

Kittal hurried through the house calling for Canaan. The servant appeared and Kittal stopped to say, "I've broken it. I've got to go and make another one. If I'm not back in three days come and find me. Also the Suwars will be here in the next few days."

Lulizen stared in the direction Kittal had headed in. Tania appeared looking cheerful. Seeing Canaan's worried face and biting his bottom lip she asked with fear, "what's happened?"

"He has gone to make a new bracelet."

"Don't you forget that he is out there." She said sternly.

"I won't." He replied, though he was sure to forget knowing that he had lots to do before the Suwars arrived. He hurried away before Tania could say any more, mentally making a list of jobs to be done as he did. Lulizen turned to Tania, "why does he need to create the bracelet? Why does he have it?"

"It's very important. If he doesn't have it he has power over life and death, but it eats away at the body. Our bodies aren't strong enough to contain all that power. It is too much for the body to handle that is why the most powerful and dangerous magics are put away in his bracelet. He would end up dead in forty-eight hours if he didn't. He doesn't like having all that power but it goes with being Nejus of the Dragons. He doesn't know how to control all of it. None of our ancestors have ever been able to apart from the first."

He headed in the opposite direction to the temple to a small place carved into the rock face high on the valley side. There was a hole in the roof, above a font filled with rainwater. Reaching it Kittal took everything out of his bag and arranged them in order. He opened the book he had brought along to a well-thumbed page. He set the book, open to the page, on the floor in front of him. He striped what clothes he wore apart from his trousers. He knelt on the floor and bowed towards the small statue of the Dragon God. It glared out across the valley from its small alcove. It had painted flames rising up around its hind legs and tail.

Kittal spent the rest of the day bowing towards the statue, muttering words of devotion and asking for assistance in the recreation of his bracelet. He continued on through the night by the light of the moon as it shone through the hole in the roof of the cave.

As the sun rose up to begin a new day Kittal stood, stretching his limbs. He washed his body down with the cold rainwater before settling to mediate, purifying his body and mind for the next day. In his mind he went to a desolate area of desert where there was nothing for miles, a place for deep thought.

He was ready to go to sleep by the evening, but he forced himself to stay awake. He was waiting for his Dragon Overlord to come to him and tell him that he could go on to the next stage. He wished the God would hurry up since he could feel the power inside him beginning to harm him. He prayed through the night, trying to prove that he was worthy of a visit. A cold breeze blew through, but he ignored it though every bone of his body was feeling chilled.

Dawn of a new day arrived with still no indication that he could progress further. His scars hurt and he could feel the blood beginning to dribble down his cheek and back. He wiped it away as he prepared for another day of mediation. As he washed his body he glanced up and saw the statue glowing red in its alcove. Kittal bowed even lower, his forehead touching the roughly hewed floor. From the statue came a deep voice, *"you have shown great patience, one that I only saw in the first High Priest. You have waited long enough and you have a great deal to do in this world yet. The time has come when you need all of the ancient powers within you. Set to and make the mix, this evening when it is ready I will speak again."*

"Yes O Great One but I will not last that long. My body as a vessel for all this power is not strong enough and it is already failing." He remembered his father dying when the man thought he could contain the powers of the Dragon God in his body.

His father had trained and prepared for years and thought himself ready, but it wasn't to be. He wasn't the one and had never become Nejus. He remembered his grandfather just laughing at his father's failed attempt and hadn't even bothered to mourn him. His eye was already on his eldest grandson as an heir to be proud of. His mother had had to organise the burial of her husband as she saw her eldest two taken from her. As if reading his thoughts the voice said, *"it was not your father's destiny, it is yours. Your heart is strong and pure. Your body will survive"* The voice said with confidence, *"till this evening."*

Having no wish to anger the God Kittal set about making up the mix that normally was used to create the vessels. With a spell he set the rainwater in the font simmering. As the day went by he added the different powders and dried plants to the quietly bubbling water. His blood was still running out of his scars and down his face, neck and back due to the more dominant power inside pushing it out to make way for itself. There was nothing he could do about it as he grew weaker.

With the evening he knelt on the floor believing that the God had tricked him into death. He tried to wipe the blood away from his scar but only smeared it across his cheek. He was preparing for his death when the statue spoke, *"you are strong, which is what you and your family will need in the time to come."*

"Thank you Great One." Kittal murmured weakly.

"Don't give up on yourself just yet." Out of nowhere a dragon's large claw appeared holding a gold goblet. The claw dipped the goblet into the font and brought it up full of the liquid mix Kittal had made. The claw held it out as the voice said, *"drink all of it in one go and then you will be ready for what is to come. It will line your body so that you can contain all that great power within you and therefore learn to control it and save this world. Drink now."*

Cautiously Kittal took the goblet from the claw which then instantly vanished. He took a deep breath to still his jittering nerves. He lifted the goblet to his lips and drank all that it contained. Not one drop was in his mouth for more than a second

As the mix began to work he dropped the goblet. He clutched his stomach, which felt like it was on fire and his face screwed up from the burning pain. He could feel the blood rushing through his body to the weakest parts, his scars. They broke open with the sudden influx of escaping blood. The steady dribble from his scars turned to what felt like a raging torrent. The agony was too much for him to bear and he fainted away on the floor of the carved-out chamber.

Canaan knew he had forgotten something important when the Suwars arrived and there was no Kittal to welcome them. He couldn't believe he had forgotten about his Nejus when he realised what it was he had forgotten. The fastest way to get to his Lord was by dragon. He crossed over to where Ciara was getting off her dragon, wearing the clothes of a dragon rider and the cloth headdress of a Suwar held on by a leather knotted strap. She looked around and when Canaan reached her asked, "where is Kittal?"

"He went to make a new bracelet but has yet to return. He said he would be here."

Suddenly afraid Ciara climbed back on to her dragon saying to it, *"we're going to find the Nejus. It is important we find him."*

"I understand Ciara." The dragon replied solemnly as it rose into the air before the rider had even got back into her saddle.

She knew where to find Kittal and directed her dragon straight towards the rock chamber, afraid that she would find her older brother dead. Her dragon hovered close to the opening of the manmade cave while Ciara got off, landing on her feet lightly. Though the dragon blocked most of the light she spotted Kittal by the sunlight coming in from the hole in the roof. She knelt at his side noticing the blood that covered him and the floor. Around his body was a flickering golden aura of power. Feeling her touch he moaned softly and tried to move. Ciara said, "don't move Kittal, I'll get you back to the house."

She dragged Kittal across the floor to the large opening. To her dragon she said, *"let me get back on and then we'll take the Nejus down. Carry him carefully."*

The quiet dragon nodded her head in understanding as Ciara climbed back into her saddle. It gently took hold of Kittal in one of its forearm claws before heading down to the house, carrying the Nejus of the Dragons carefully but firmly.

The three back at the house didn't know what to say. To Canaan Ciara ordered, "get some warm water and get it to his room."

The dragon place Kittal on the ground as Canaan jogged away to do as Ciara had ordered. With Tania's help Ciara got Kittal into the house. He only just walked in with their help. His feet dragged on the floor occasionally. His eyes were barely open and if they closed another drop of blood wept out from his tear ducts. He was washed of his blood before they put him to bed. By then the flow of blood had nearly stopped. He was weak from the loss and lay in bed with his head resting on his scar free right cheek. He occasionally grimaced in his near unconscious state.

Four women watched over his as Kittal slowly regained his strength. They talked quietly amongst themselves as they took it in turns to cool his feverish brow. Over his restlessly sleeping body Ciara said with a smile to Lulizen, "he mentioned you have agreed to join with him." Lulizen nodded.

"Has he told you what will happen at the ceremony?" Ciara asked, wondering if Lulizen knew what she was letting herself in for. She thought there was a fragility to Lulizen though she came across strong. She wondered what her brother saw in her. One thing for sure she preferred Lulizen to Kittal's first wife.

"No, but I'm guessing it will be similar to the ceremony we had at my family home." Lulizen hesitantly guessed.
Ciara rolled her eyes, "like a typical man he has left it to the women to tell you the details." With a tight smile she went on, "there are vows in a private ceremony amongst family but there is more. Dragons mate for life like us. When they join together the male forces himself on his chosen female, dominating her."

"What has that got to do with Kittal and me?" Lulizen asked with worry as the older woman paused.

"In front of his peers, any couple where one or both of them are connected to the noble breed of Dragons must do as they do. In front of us he will force himself on you. It is one custom we have not been able to rid ourselves of as the dragons do like their traditions."

Lulizen looked horrified. She shook in her shock. Tania took the younger woman into her arms as her aunt went on, "I'm sorry you have to know, it would have been worse if you hadn't known at all. You just have to ignore the people watching you and Kittal. No one likes to do it, especially when the man really loves his woman. I hated it. Once was enough. I've already told him to be gentle on you and I think he would anyway, whether I had said anything or not." She tried to smile at Lulizen but it just came out as a sorry look since she knew what it was like, "be strong, you'll have to hope you never have to go through it again as once you are linked with the dragons you are so for life. You are at a disadvantage from Her since you haven't lived with our customs."

Lulizen sat silent as she wondered what she had let herself in for. But then she realised now was the time to ask questions she knew Kittal would not answer. She wanted to know more about his first wife and learn from her mistakes. She cautiously asked, "who is She? Everyone occasionally mentions her but never says anymore."

Ciara glanced at her niece and own daughter who was a similar age to Lulizen. Both had become attentive, wanting to hear as well. Tania always wanted any little scrap of information about her mother. Ciara wanted to reveal the truth but didn't want to scare Lulizen or spoil whatever image Tania had of her mother.

"Her name was Abbitha and she was my brother's first wife. Deep down he still loves her though I never could. He would never hurt her." Ciara glanced at Tania again, remembering the year Kittal has spent agonising over whether Tania was his daughter or Titan's. She was unsure how to say the next bit, "she died in a terrible accident." She stood taking the three young women by surprise and left the room.

She couldn't do it; couldn't lie. It was safer to leave the room and hope none of them asked for any more information.

Abbitha had wanted the best of both worlds. She had had both brothers under her spell. She wanted the title but the other brother. Kittal foolishly forgave her the first few times she had slept with Titan. The last time was too much. He had caught them in her bed while their two-year-old daughter slept nearby. He had hid in the shadows watching with growing anger with tears rolling down his face. He watched as she ached her back and moaned softly at Titan's tender touches. She clung to Titan as he drew her on to his lap and she allowed him to enter her. Her naked legs wrapped around Titan's hips and her fingers dug into Titan's back. Kittal had left then.

Ciara remembered having to calm her raging brother and was there when Kittal had ordered Abbitha into his presence. Abbitha had fallen to her knees when she had seen Kittal's stony face and the upper ranks of the Suwars around the temple. She heard the dragons growling around her. She had tried to look remorseful, but nothing could hide the glint of secret pleasures performed. She sneered, "I know you won't hurt me."

Kittal had said nothing as he had crouched down before her. He stared deep into her face making Abbitha nervous. Before she could move his hands shot out and grabbed her round the throat. His grip tightened as he stood, rising her into the air. She scrabbled to get his hands away as she felt her last breath leave her. He dropped her and she landed with a thud. He walked away without looking back.

Ciara had stared in astonishment and had reached for her husband's hand as if reassuring him she wouldn't do what Abbitha had done. She hadn't thought he would really do it considering how young they all were but clearly their grandfather had taught him well in being a man in full control of everything including his own wife's life. None of them had. Titan had left the valley the following day.

Ciara was called back to Kittal's room. She rushed in to find that Kittal had stirred. He had rolled on to his side, his hand hanging over the side of the bed. He slowly opened his eyes as he felt someone's hand on his own. He smiled softly, though he hadn't worked out who was looking at him, and then he grimaced. Tania climbed on to the bed. Ciara sat on the edge of the bed smiling down at her brother while Lulizen hung by her side. Ciara said to him, "welcome back to the world brother, what were you doing in that place apart from making a new vessel?"

"He gave it to me." Kittal mumbled.

"Gave what to you?" Ciara asked looking confused.

"I have it all, all the powers of the Nejus and they are all within me. I can cope with them and use them."

"What does that mean for us?"

"I can rescue the dragons now." He smiled sleepily.

"What dragons Kittal? What about Titan? Kittal?"
He had fallen back to sleep. Ciara turned to Tania and Lulizen, "what was he talking about?"

"I don't know." Tania frowned. She looked to Lulizen, "has he said anything to you?"

"Only that he needs the Suwars to help him rescue some dragons." Lulizen carefully said.

"I'll get it out of him when he is well and then we will all know. He had to have got those scars on his back from wherever these dragons are. It's like he has been whipped." Ciara remarked to the others, "now, I believe we have a dress to make." She smiled up at Lulizen.

Thirteen

Both of them were nervous, though for Kittal it was the second time. He glanced round, seeing all the eyes watching in the last light of the evening. The Suwars were there in their ceremonial metal armour. Kittal wore one of his red robes over a shirt and trousers. His hair had been trimmed for the occasion and a medallion hung at his chest.

The dragons were behind them and all the way round the temple and on the cliffs above, clutching the edges. They looked solemnly down and if they caught Kittal's eye they closed their own and gave him a vague nod of encouragement. He turned back to Lulizen and gave her a smile of reassurance. He took her hands in his, giving them a squeeze as he did.

Lulizen gazed into his eyes and forgot about the audience as she saw love written in his grey eyes. She decided to just think about the private ceremony they had had an hour earlier where he had promised to worship her, protect her and care for her for all of his life. She gave him a smile as he smiled at her.

She wore a veil over her plaited hair which fell down her back and floated in the breeze. The dress she wore was made of silk with a flounced skirt hiding her bare feet. It was pulled tight at her waist. The square necked bodice was so low that her breasts threatened to pop out. She wore a necklace of sapphires, produced by Kittal that morning, the necklace of the Nejus' wife. A jewelled ring was already on her wedding finger as part of the morning's private ceremony. Bangles were on her wrists and similar round her ankles, jingling if she moved slightly.

She closed her eyes as Kittal put his hands on her head, holding it still. She didn't want to know what he was going to do. He licked his dry lips and then kissed her. His hands dropped from her head and slipped down her body. He picked her up and she wrapped her legs round him as the kisses moved down to her cleavage. She found her back pressed up against a pillar as she wrapped her arms round Kittal. She felt him enter her and her mouth opened to protest but no sound came out. She realised it felt good in a strange way as it was so different from how they normally showed their love.

She didn't see the gold glow around him as the power of the Dragon God surged through him and into Lulizen. The dragons murmured to themselves in surprise. Until then none of them knew what had occurred between their Lord Defender and their ancient ancestor. They wondered what was to come if the great power had been bestowed on Kittal.

Both were gasping for breath as he put her down and she opened her eyes. She felt different inside, as if their growing child had absorbed some of his father's power and strength in the process of penetration. He gave her a shy smile. Lulizen reached up and gave him a kiss making him sigh with relief that she wasn't angry at him for what had just happened.

From behind them clapping began and people rose to their feet to cross the cracked floor of the temple to congratulate the couple. Ciara and her eldest and Canaan with an arm round Tania led the way across. Ciara kissed both Lulizen and Kittal while smiling. The Suwars behind the family bowed in their respect. Ciara remarked, "a child now perhaps?"

"Perhaps." Kittal murmured as he nuzzled Lulizen's neck, kissing it, not revealing their little secret. She smiled in embarrassment and shrugged his head away.

On the house lawn the villagers had set up the tables to celebrate with the Suwars and the family. A select few from Linyee looked lost amongst the bawdy banter of the villagers.

Lulizen and Kittal sat at the head of the table on the cushions that were strewn around from when people had been eating. The lit torches flickered in the wind as a selection of Suwars demonstrated the acrobatics that they all learnt as part of their training. They leapt over their dragons or got flung into the air by their rides flicking their tails and somersaulting before landing on the dragon's backs.

Lulizen leant against Kittal with half closed eyes. He murmured, "this night isn't over yet."

"I know." She replied softly. She glanced up as he put one arm round her and picked up his goblet to drink from with the other. Putting it down he rubbed his scar softly as he sat thinking about other things, though his mind should have been on Lulizen. Now that the ceremony had been done and he knew she was pregnant he wanted to be off, leading the Suwars to free the dragons calling out for help in his dreams.

They were asleep when Canaan rushed into the tent. He was relieved to find his master and new mistress asleep. He shook Kittal awake saying, "Nejus, quick."

Kittal turned away from Canaan, putting an arm over the naked Lulizen. Canaan shook him even harder, "please wake up Nejus, its Kite."

Kittal stirred and groggily asked as he opened his eyes, "what Canaan?"

"Her egg is opening sir."

Kittal's eyes widened and he reached for his scattered clothes. He disturbed Lulizen who pulled a sheet up in her embarrassment of having Canaan in the tent. She saw Kittal getting dressed, "what's going on?"

"Kite's egg is hatching, I must go. Come, stay or go back to the house."

She hesitated before saying; "I'll see you back at the house."

He bent down and gave her a quick peck, "see you there, come on Canaan." He headed out of the tent and deeper into the valley to the majority of the dragons' nests.

He led the way, knowing where he was going. The gathered dragons parted enough to allow him through. Kite glanced up briefly and then returned to watching her egg. Cracks had appeared in the shell and there were the sounds of them being produced from within. Kittal knelt by the side of the egg, his eyes wide and hardly blinking. He reached out nervously and touched the mottled shell. He felt the little dragon move within and smiled. He left his hand there as guidance for the creature trying to get out.

There was a loud crack and a small claw on a wing appeared close to Kittal's hand and clung to the edge of the shell. Kittal moved his hand so that the dragon inside could hold it and know that the flesh it held was its Nejus'. It was slimy to the feel as it was covered in yolk, Kittal didn't notice since he had done it many times before. Another small claw appeared and then the round pointed top of the large egg cracked all the way round. The small claw let go of Kittal. His eyes moved to the top of the egg and he saw it lift upwards. He took it off and the small Dragon blinked in the sun and gazed round unsure of where it was. Kittal smiled and whispered, *"it's all right little one, out you come."*

The little dragon attempted to climb out of its shell, but it only resulted in the shell falling over. It crawled out on all fours and blinked rapidly. It did a full 360 turn, looking at all there was around it. It tried to flap its wings, but they were still covered in the yolk that had protected and fed it while it had been in the shell. It opened its mouth and squeaked, nothing like the roar that it would be able to do once it was fully grown. Kittal couldn't help smiling again as it took a step forward and toppled over, unused to walking. Kite bent down and sniffed her child, checking that it was real. Deciding it was hers she gave the soft scales of the infant a lick of her tongue. She glanced over at Kittal as if asking to know if she was doing it right. He said to her look, *"keep*

going, your instincts are right. Look after it for she will be my son's."
Kite appeared to smile and then went back to cleaning the female dragon. Kittal gave her a pat and then headed away, knowing that the dragons would want to do their own celebrating.

Kittal headed homewards with a smile on his face. It slipped when he saw Ciara standing on the veranda looking serious. He asked with concern, "what's wrong?"

"Now it is time to talk."

She glanced at Canaan as he slipped away.

"Walk with me then?"

She joined him at the bottom of the steps and together they walked out into the valley. He asked, "what do you want to know?"

"Everything. You have talked of rescuing dragons."

"Have I?" He looked surprised.

Ciara sighed. He was already trying to deflect. She remarked, "you went searching for blood and knowledge."

"And I found both." He smiled at her, "I found the desert dragons alive and well but they knew nothing of any renegade Suwars. However they knew of dragon colonies in the mountains and off the coast."

Fourteen

After having asked Titan to look after Keytel Kittal had travelled to the rocky desert which lay far to the north in the rain shadow of the mountains of Gloabtona, through the enclosed high steppe plains of Moronland. He recalled visiting the country when he had been younger with a smile having found women and dragons high on a lone mountaintop. He smiled at the girl he had spent time with. But remembering the state of their dragons was the reason he was searching for new blood. He didn't want the Valley's dragons to go the same way and now Tania was old enough it was time to go seeking new blood from any surviving dragon tribes.

He found himself in a landscape where the wind and water had created rocky sandstone stacks and smooth sided canyons from flash floods. He walked the canyons for several days searching for evidence of the desert dragons. He found the old tracks of one and carefully followed its tail drag until it joined up with others. They led into the ground, into an old sink hole. He slid down the ramp of sand and came up against the body of a dragon.

The ochre coloured dragon turned, its frill rising up to scare the intruder off. It demanded, *"who goes there?"* Its eyes narrowed against the sunlight streaming down the hole. It curled his tail around Kittal, drawing the man closer. Behind the dragon Kittal saw several more heads rise up to see what was happening. He couldn't see how deep the hole was nor how many dragons there were within it. They walked on short legs and were more like lizards than dragons as most were wingless.

"I do not mean you harm." Kittal bowed.

"You are not afraid of us? You speak our language?" The dragon asked in surprise.

"Where I come from I am the lord and defender of your kind."

"I have heard tell of this. One of us left a long time ago to find out more. He never returned."

"Nefrent? He chose to be my grandfather's dragon. It was him who scarred my face." Kittal briefly thought back to the time when he had been ten years old.

He and Ciara, who had been showing unusual promise for a girl, were just finishing a few days with their mother and brother. Neither had wanted to go back to their grandfather in Linyee as he was a scary disciplinarian. The day before they were due to fly to Linyee with his grandfather, who had come to fetch them, Nefrent had cornered him. Kittal had frozen to the spot as he knew Nefrent had a temper. Each eyed the other warily before Nefrent spoke, *"come closer."*

When the boy didn't respond the dragon reached out and knocked him over. He pinned the boy down, *"I didn't come all this way for nothing to be indentured to a man. You are important to our future even if you don't know it."*

Kittal stared up in fear and confusion, *"what do you mean?"*

"I can see into the future and you have a destiny to fulfil. Your ancestor has finally been reincarnated in you."

"I don't understand."

"Stop your questions boy. There are those that need to be saved, but they will need to know."

Kittal's eyes grew wider and he fought the dragon's hold as the sandy coloured dessert dragon pressed a claw against his cheek. He screamed as the claw broke through his skin and tore through his flesh. He had fainted away then. Even with the wound his grandfather had taken him away from the valley with the gruff remark, "best get you ready for your destiny."

"There would have been a reason. I have heard tell of a man scarred like you who once visited us."

Curious Kittal asked, *"my ancestor. What did he want?"*

"That was not passed down. What do you want from us?"

"Knowledge and blood. My dragons are becoming inbred and we need new blood. I also seek some Suwars. It is told by my people that some left to create a new colony."

"None came here and nor will you take any of our children."

"I do not wish to take anyone." Kittal spoke up so those behind the dragon would hear, *"I am offering the chance to visit and be a guest in my valley."*

There was movement further in the hole. The dragon leader turned and snapped at a young dragon trying to approach. He hissed, *"step back. You are going nowhere!"*

The young winged dragon reluctantly shuffled backwards. Kittal was disappointed that the dragon had such control over his colony. He hoped that come the evening at least one dragon would ignore their leader. He bowed, *"I thank you for listening."*

"I wish you luck in your search." The dragon bowed his head. He watched suspiciously as Kittal left. No man would ever tame any one of his tribal members.

Kittal camped on a ridge keeping a discreet eye on the dragons' cool home. He felt sure one of them would rebel if he was patient enough. He didn't have to wait long for the dragons to climb out of their hole, sniffing the air. Satisfied, they went their separate ways.

One paused longer than the rest, waiting for its companions to disappear off hunting. With them gone it flew up to the rocky ledge where Kittal sat. Kittal rose, *"welcome."*

"I would like to see your valley."

"You are welcome any time and they will welcome you."

Kittal smiled.

The dragon glanced round and lowered her voice, *"go to the coast. There is a tribe there. They need your help."*

Kittal frowned, *"what do you mean?"*

"You'll find out. I must go."

"Maybe I will see you again one day. Thank you."

"Us wild ones are slowly shrinking in number. I hope you'll be able to protect us as well as you have the ones in your care already."

"I will do all I can." Kittal remarked solemnly.

"Thank you." The dragon bowed her head as Kittal bowed. He watched as the dragon flew off, pushing off the soft stone. He decided to stay the night and make his way to the coast in the morning.

Having made his way north to the desert he now found himself heading south east, across the lowlands of the Mountains of Gloabtona. He walked across heavily forested lands punctuated with a few small villages ignored by the surrounding countries. It was a wild landscape but with few signs of dragons.

He headed for the coast as suggested by the desert dragon. In this remote corner of Keytel was the lawless port city of Senspanta which ran itself without interference from anyone and if anyone tried to make their mark they were scorned. This was a city Titan should be ruling over as acting Governor of the northern lands of Keytel but even he had left them be.

Standing on a ridgeline above the city Kittal wondered what he would find. Though he was Nejus and flown over most of Keytel he couldn't recall much of the city. He felt sure Keytel saw little of its wealth. In face most of it was shared with Jukirla. He considered investigating that once he returned home.

Senspanta spread out either side of the mouth of the meandering River Sens with two bridges connecting the two sides together. Large seawalls created a sheltered harbour against the winter storms. At the end of one seawall was a large lighthouse which lit up the harbour in the darkening sky. From the ridge the island of Jukirla with its mountains could be seen on the horizon, a two-day journey by boat.

The streets were lined with stone and timber buildings in various stages of repair and wealth. The streets themselves were bustling with people trading openly on the streets or in awning covered shopfronts, as Kittal weaved his way through them in search of a room for the night. He barely got a glance which for him was a novelty, but he wasn't the only one who had been in one too many fights. It was the sort of place that it was safer not to reveal who he really was.

He placed gold on the countertop. The innkeeper, a slim well-groomed man, remarked out of curiosity, "with that sort of money you are here for something."
Kittal looked thoughtful, trying to decide if he could reveal what he wanted, "I am looking for some creatures, dragons."

"Every newcomer hopes to see one of those." The innkeeper chuckled as the money disappeared from the countertop before Kittal could reclaim it, "there are none here. You have to go to Jukirla for them. There are plenty of them there though they'll cost you. You looking to use them?"

"Yes." Kittal decided was the safe answer.

"If you want to see one then you'll need to go down to the docks. One of their ships is due in tomorrow and if you want to cross to the island you might get passage on it."

"Thank you."

He was down on the docks early but kept to the shadows and out of the way of the labourers emptying and loading the ships already dockside. Behind him was a large brick building where men holding papers were standing on the steps as they waited for the doors to open for another day of trade. Large windows gave the hall inside plenty of light and tables were ranged down one side to aid in the signing of contracts.

As another ship came into view he headed to the end of the seawall. He watched in shock and disbelief as he saw that the galley was being pulled by a sea dragon. How did he not know about this? Titan should have been reporting such things back to him.

Its mouth was chained shut as its head dipped above the water and then back down as it pulled the loaded galley through the waves. Linked to a separate chain round her neck were two more lengths of chain which were anchored to the deck of the galley ship. The chains went slack as it came into harbour. Oars came out of the holes that ran down each side of the boat and they pulled the boat into harbour.

Sensing Kittal's presence it turned its head briefly before disappearing under the water with a wave of its tail. The eye that had stared at him recognised him but looked mournful as well. Kittal gave it a nod of acknowledgement. He knew now he needed to find out more.

He didn't want to aid them in their abuses of dragons but he needed to get to Jukirla. Reluctantly he approached the captain of the ship and purchased passage although it wouldn't be till the following morning.

Kittal waited till the evening when the harbour emptied of labourers and the crew of the galley had gone into the city for drink and women. He sat on the edge of the quay as the galley rocked on its anchor lines. He glanced round before drawing out his bracelet from a pocket of his new oilcloth coat. Compared to the rest of Keytel it was cold and raining, the raindrops rippling the calm water of the harbour.

He stripped down to his underwear and slipped into the chilly water, bracelet on his wrist. The powers within seeped through his skin allowing him to breath underwater as he dived down. He followed the keel of the galley down till he reached the bottom where the sea dragon drifted.

It stopped slowly turning when it felt Kittal's presence. It shook its head. Kittal swam across. He ran his hands over the chains round its snout searching for a weak link to break. Finding one he pulled at it one handed, the hand with the bracelet on, till it broke. With another shake of its head and a snap of its jaws the chains loosened and sank to the seabed, *"thank you Nejus."*

"You know who I am?"

"We have been waiting for your arrival so you can save us."

"Are you all chained up?"

The Sea dragon nodded, *"we were enslaved a long time ago by those who claimed to be our protectors."*

"I cannot promise anything."

"Just see how we are suffering at least." She said with fear that he wouldn't help them.

"I am coming back with you. I should go before my clothes are stolen from the quay."

"Go. May the Dragon Lord support you in our rescue."

When the galley was ready to leave in the morning the sea dragon rebelled, going for the dramatic rather than slipping away during the night. She twisted and turned till the chain slipped over her head and she could then swim through them and away. Kittal, at the bow of the ship, smiled as he watched the eel like dragon leap out of the sea at the mouth of the harbour with a roar before diving deep. There was an answering roar as the crew ran to the side and the captain raged. He didn't understand how the dragon had escaped and now he would be in for it when he got back to Jukirla. He shouted at the crew, "get to those oars now!"

The galley sailed into the harbour, two days later than planned, passing a chain netted enclosure where sea dragons listlessly circled on one side and dry docks on the other where a new galley was being built. Wooden warehouses with wide open doors lined the back of the quays. The port of Jukir was busy with huge slow-moving carts filled with rock and metal ore being pulled by dragons the size of the largest carthorses, wrapped in chains, passing through to the places where they would be processed or sold on. The chains were covered in mud and dried black blood from where they rubbed on their scales. Their wings were tied down and their mouths chained shut like the sea dragon's had been. Kittal fought back tears as he saw them being so abused. Where had the ethics of the Suwars gone? What had happened to cause them to enslave dragons? He felt the beaded bracelet on his wrist vibrate but knew it was too soon to show his intentions.

Port officials were down on the quayside as Kittal disembarked. They blocked his way with their white sticks, marks of their authority. They eyed him suspiciously, "who are you? Why are you visiting Jukir and Jukirla?"

"I am a man of wealth here to spend money." Kittal lied. Their eyes lit up. No man can resist when money is involved. One asked, "what are you after?"

"I have heard you are renown for your industries and was hoping to tour them. What are these beasts?"

"You do not know what they are?" The man was surprised, "they are our dragons. We use them instead of horses. They are a lot stronger and last longer." The man said with pride and then with a warning added, "you can't have any. They are not for sale."

Before Kittal could respond the conversation further down the quay distracted everyone.

The owner of the galley and the captain were gesticulating at each other and the galley. The owner was heard shouting, "how could the fucking beast get away?! There has never been a dragon that escaped."

"Maybe the chains had a weak link. They are crafty fuckers."

"They were new chains." The owner exclaimed.

"Be glad it didn't turn on the ship and sink it."

"I'm going to have to train another now. As for you, don't think you'll be allowed back on any of my ships. Get your stuff and go."

Over Kittal's shoulder the port official said, "don't worry sir. Our dragons have never escaped and harmed anyone. We have been doing this for a long time now."

"How long?"

"Ever since our ancestors came to this island. You should head up to the Governor's House and let him know you are here. He'll put you in touch with the right people."

"Thank you." Kittal slung his rucksack over his shoulder.

The port official watched Kittal walk off in the direction he had pointed in. He thought to himself that the man had been a curious one. He certainly didn't look like a rich merchant. Where were his servants? How can he have not known about their dragons? Now the Governor could decide what to do with him.

Kittal walked up the hill away from the docks. The further he went the more gentile it became. The crowded filthy streets of the old quarter were the homes and workshops of the traders, pressed close together and overhanging the road. Out on the outskirts of the city were the heavy industries, supplying the traders with the raw goods they needed. The middle of the city was surprisingly green, made up of several large farms and orchards.

Towards the top of the hill where the air was clearer and cleaner were the homes of merchants and owners of most of the land with large gardens hidden by high walls. The houses had tall three or four storey frontages to enable the merchants to have offices at the top with telescopes so they could see what was going on further down the hill. Two wide roads traversed across the city splitting it into three.

The Governor's House was situated just under the crest of the hill which in turn was on the lower slopes of one of three mountains that dominated the island. Large balconies overlooked the large courtyard in front of it and the city below. Double doors led into a central chamber which was where petitioners were milling around or making deals with a shake of hands. Behind another set of double doors was the Governor's audience chamber.

As Kittal entered the antechamber he realised that he was under-dressed compared to everyone else. Dressed in his trousers, simple red tunic and sailcloth coat he was stared at. Before him the merchants were dressed in tailored coats and waistcoats and bleached white shirts and shoes with stockings up to their knees. They reminded Kittal of his peacocks and fought back a laugh.

A horn was sounded and the double doors to the audience chamber opened. A steward stepped out with a list and called out, "Merchant Carye."
A smug fat man whose clothes were straining around his stomach appeared and waddled forward. A tall slim man near to Kittal remarked to no one in particular, "damn it. How does he do it? I was definitely first on that list this morning. I'm never going to be able to shift my wood at this rate."

"Come on, you know he pays the steward." Another man dressed in green and with a spectacular curling moustache answered.
Kittal turned to them, "excuse me, what is going on?"
The two men glanced at each other before the tall man answered, "if you want an audience with Governor Monzanin you have to come early and be put on the list. May I ask where you are from Sir? You aren't dressed like us." He looked Kittal up and down.

"From far away. I got sent up here to talk to the Governor. I'm looking to organise a new trade link."

"Well, that's easy." The moustached man grinned, "the name's Tomas Witt and this is Bonn Smythman. Let's leave this place; Carye is going to hog what's left of the morning. Come with us. You'll get better contacts down in the shop. What's your name?"

"Kittal."

"A pleasure to meet you. Seen our dragons yet?" Bonn Smythman replied with an outstretched hand.

"Err... Yes." Kittal hid his disgust as he shook the man's hand.

"Brilliant things. I own a few myself on the other side of Jukirla. I'm only here for business, making sure my wagon of wood gets a fair price."

They left the Governor's home and headed back into the city and off the main thoroughfare to a small inn. A waiter brought them tankards of warm beer and plates of bread cheese and ham. Bonn and Tomas did most of the talking with Kittal listening and occasionally replying to questions. By the end of the afternoon he was invited back to Bonn's estate.

The journey took three days to get to Bonn's estate. They travelled through woods and fields and passed one of several mines that went deep into the mountains. Bonn's house was small in comparison to the surrounding buildings of his timber business and the piles of timber sawn and raw waiting to be sold. The road leading up to the clearing was surrounded by rows of trees of various ages. Bonn, sitting in the carriage opposite Kittal remarked with pride, "all this is mine. What do you think?"

Kittal didn't respond straight away as he was watching a dragon moving between two rows of trees pulling several tree trunks behind it. It turned its head as if it could sense Kittal.

Bonn leant forward and eagerly asked, "what do you think of it all?"

"Why do you enslave the dragons?"

Bonn shrugged, "it's what we have always done. What a strange question."

"I'm sorry. I'm still getting use to the dragons." Kittal lied, "this is all very impressive. How many do you have?"

"About ten and a few growing."

"You breed them?"

"Got to keep the blood stock going and someone always needs some new stock. They are worth a lot. I'll let you get up close to them later if you want."

"No, that's all right." Kittal turned away to look at Bonn.

Bonn's family jumped on him as he got out of the carriage. He hugged all five of his children before he was allowed to greet his wife who was dressed in a shirt with rolled up sleeves and a long skirt with a wide belt that circled her waist. She smiled lovingly at him and then saw Kittal at the door of the carriage, "who is this Bonn?"

"Oh, this is Kittal. He's from somewhere…" He realised he hadn't asked, and it was a bit late now, "he's here looking to make some deals. He looked a bit lost in town so I invited him over." He turned to his guest, "this, Kittal, is my beautiful wife Katrine."

"Madam." Kittal bowed his head.

"Welcome to the Smythman Estate." She smiled warmly at her husband's guest, "please come in and we'll squeeze you in somewhere."

The children crowded round Kittal as he followed their mother into the house. Seeing them reminded him of Tania when she was little and for a brief moment he wished he was back home.

They enjoyed a noisy dinner that reminded Kittal of when he was younger and in the Valley with his mother, brother and sister. The family love and joy had come when he was allowed to visit his mother and his siblings in the valley. It was why he had made his home in the valley when he took over from his grandfather as Nejus. Thinking about it all made him realise it was time he found a new wife to be-get the heir he needed.

He waited for the house to fall silent before slipping out and across the clearing to a path that led to the dragons. Kittal found the dragons pinned to the ground and was surprised, now that he was so close to them, how small they were compared to his healthy ones in the valley. Over time they had shrunk from their poor diet and treatment. They turned their heads as much as they could at his approach.

He walked through them till he found their nominated leader. He bowed, *I never thought to see such noble beasts enslaved."*

The eyes of the dragon slowly closed and opened.

"Let me loosen these chains so we can talk." He had his bracelet on his wrist and stretched the chains around the dragon's snout. He then ran his hands over the sores, healing them and watched it as the healing spread outwards from his hands.

The dragon stretched its jaw before saying, *"thank you. Come closer so I can see you."*

Kittal held his wrist up and the power within the bracelet caused it to glow and the dragon was then able to see him, *"I am Kittal, Nejus of Keytel and the dragons of my realm."*

"You are scarred."

"I am. It was one of your own who did it to me. He said that one day it would be of use to me."

"It has been passed down that a man with the scar you have would come and free us and here you are."

"Free you? I would love to but I can not. I am not strong enough to. I am here on my own. Why have none of you tried to free yourselves? How did you end up like this?"

"We have tried many times over the centuries but our bonds just got tighter. Some have kinder owners than others. Those at the mine and quarries have it the worst. Those they consider troublesome or too old are sent there."

"And here?"

"He is reasonable. Some of his overseers can be cruel but no crueller than any one of us can be."

"And how did you end up like this? One of the desert tribe suggested that the Suwars I am looking for came here."

"They did. Those that came here quickly overpowered our ancestors. We had rarely seen man at that point. The small wild ones and theirs mixed creating what you see today."

She turned her head, *"there is someone else here."*

The dragons tried to look as Kittal stepped away and wished he had his knife with him, but it was hidden in his bag. He moved through the dragons and was surprised to find a twelve-year-old hiding behind the tail of one of them. Kittal grabbed him by the arm and demanded, "why are you here? Were you following me?"

The blonde-haired boy stared wide eyed at Kittal, "you were talking to them?"

Kittal softened a little, "I was."

"How?"

"Where I come from they are free and I look after them." He paused as he considered what to say next and to recall the boy's name, "Arno, I need to ask something of you. I need this to be our secret. Can you manage that?"

The boy carefully nodded and then asked, "don't they hurt anyone?"

"No. I protect both man and dragon. Now, you'd best head back before you are found missing. Actually; wait a minute." Kittal left the boy and returned to the dragon. He put a hand on her shoulder, *"I'm going to have to tighten the chains again so they don't know that I have been here. I'll be back."* The dragon nodded. Kittal, with a heavy sigh, put his hands on the chains and felt them tighten.

He returned to Arno who asked, "how did you do that?"

"Now that is my secret." Kittal smiled.

He spent a week with the Smythmans, going out with Bonn during the day around his estate; and at night slipping out to the dragons. One by one he healed all their sores, wounds and aches till he was exhausted. Arno accompanied him a few times and asked questions, some of which Kittal answered and some he didn't.

With all the dragons healed he excused himself and disappeared deep into the woods so he could recover his strength. He felt sucked dry from healing the dragons and hearing them in his mind. It was clear they communicated with each other telepathically as their mouths were chained shut. News of his arrival had spread across the island.

Deep in the forest he spread his coat on the ground and stripped down to his trousers. He began meditating. Slowly peace returned to his spirit and the Dragon God looked benevolently down on him. His strength returned after a long day and evening of meditating and then he slept till morning wrapped in his coat.

He appeared for breakfast dressed as if he had not spent a day and night in the forest. Katrine smiled warmly at him, "are you feeling better sir?"

"A lot, thank you."

"Do you know, since you have been here our dragons have been so much easier to handle." Katrine remarked, "maybe you should stay with us."

Bonn frowned at her, "ssh, that is not our guest's concern."

"You were the one to comment." She turned on her husband.

"Yes, but it's not because he is here."

Kittal looked across at Arno who shook his head. He had said nothing. He could sense Katrine Smythman had a good idea that he was involved in the suddenly better condition of their dragons, "I think it's time I moved on. There is still plenty of Jukirla to see. Thank you for all your generous hospitality."

Bonn frowned briefly. He had hoped to organise a trade deal. Putting a brave face on it all he offered, "would you like a horse?"

"No thank you. I am used to walking."

Bonn and Katrine waved him off from the steps of their home. She remarked, "there was definitely more to him then he revealed."

"You think so."

"He was no merchant or trader Bonn. The important bit is we didn't offend him so there will be no trouble."

"I'll ask around."

"Be discreet. I don't want any repercussions."

From a bedroom window Arno watched Kittal leave. He may have only been twelve years old but he knew as soon as he could he wanted to go to Keytel and see Kittal's dragons and become a Suwar. He liked what Kittal had told him.

Fifteen

Kittal spent several months walking the roads and paths of Jukirla. He observed the use of dragons in the mines and quarries and when he could he spoke with them and healed their sores. Again and again they asked for him to help free them and there was nothing he could do.

Now he needed to get into the Governor's House. He needed to see the oldest records to see why the Suwars had turned against the dragons. He was walking up to the Governor's House as a carriage rocked past.

Within the carriage was Governor Monzanin and his son looking out of the window. The young man stared out of the window our of boredom until someone caught his eye. He leant out of the window as he watched Kittal walk up the hill. He grabbed his father's sleeve, "father, do you know who is on the island?"

"What do you mean Dunan?"

"Come look."

The Governor leant out, "who am I looking at?"

"The man with the scar on his face. He's by the apple stall."

"He's probably just a visitor. We have plenty of them come to stare at our dragons." The Governor shrugged.

"No he's not!" His son exclaimed, "that is the Nejus of Keytel. A dragon rider."

The Governor's eyes widened. For once his son's obsession with all things dragon had proven useful. It might also explain the stories going round of dragons that had been healed overnight of all their wounds. He leant out of the window and shouted at the two guards on horseback, "grab that man by the apple stall. Clap him in chains like his dragons."

Everyone turned as the two mounted soldiers rode up the road and surrounded Kittal on their skittish horses. Kittal looked up, surprised. One of the soldiers said as he got down from his horse, "you are under arrest."

"May I ask why?"

"The Governor doesn't need a reason."

Kittal briefly thought about protesting but then decided it was safer not to. Now was not the time to create a scene and potentially reveal himself as he didn't know how the people of Jukir would react. It also meant he was at least in the Governor's House.

"Come with us sir."

"Of course."

Kittal was marched up the hill to the Governor's House and to a side entrance. Steps led down to the under croft where most of the rooms were for storage. In a dark damp corner was the Governor's prison cells though they rarely held a prisoner for long. He was allowed to walk in but was then pushed up against a wall, his bag taken from him and chained to the wall.

He was kept waiting for most of the day and had no idea what time it was when the broad-shouldered Governor made his presence known with his son behind him. Kittal stood as the door opened. Governor Monzanin took a step back. The room was filled with an energy he could sense but couldn't explain. Scornfully Kittal glared at the two men.

He looked them over. Governor Monzanin had his own large presence but more through tight control of access to himself. His eyes lingering on the younger of the two who must take after his mother for he didn't look anything like his father with his slim build and delicate features. He looked more the sort who lived the life of a scholar but there was a keenness in his eyes as if he wanted his father gone so he could ask the questions his father didn't want him to ask.

Trying to regain dominance the Governor stood taller as he remarked, "so you are Nejus of Keytel?"

"I am." Kittal saw no point in lying.

The Governor's eyes narrowed. The man before him looked nothing like a ruler although he knew that the Nejus had left his brother temporarily in charge of his country, "I do not believe you. Who are you really? How dare you interfere with my property."

"What do you want me to be?" Kittal challenged.

"Whoever you are you'll soon be a nobody." Governor Monzanin sneered.

His son protested, "father, no, it is him."

"Be quiet." The Governor snapped before turning back.

"Father, he has powers that you don't know about. He could hurt you."

"Quiet!" Governor turned and shoved his son from the room. He closed the door on the young man. He glared at Kittal, "you will soon be joining other nobodies where you can't cause trouble for my island."

"You should listen to your son as you may come to regret your decision." Kittal warned.

"Are you threatening me?!" His temper was up now.

"Release me and I'll give you a year to free your dragons or I'll be back with more than just myself."

No way was Monzanin going to let his mad man threaten him. He pulled off his coat and threw it behind him. He rolled up his sleeves and stepped forward. He thumped Kittal in the stomach, forcing all the air out of Kittal's chest. Monzanin sneered, "see who's in charge now."

He hit Kittal again and again, laughing as he did. He didn't care that his son could see him doing so.

His son stared in disbelief through the barred window in the door. He had never seen this side of his father. As Kittal's head hung low he pushed the door open, "father, stop this. He hasn't done anything wrong."

"Anyone who threatens me, or our country gets to feel my fist and worst." Monzanin said to his son between breathes. It had been a while since he had hit anyone. He reached down for his coat, "come, he'll be gone by morning and will no longer be our concern."

True to his word Kittal was on his way to Monzanin's mines by morning, slumped in an empty cart with several other chained men. Dunan spent a week searching for him. He was determined to ask Kittal his own questions.

Kittal had already spent four days on the rock face in the mine digging out copper ore when Dunan found him. He was filthy, ached all over and his hands were sore even for him. Even with all this there was still an aura about him as he stood in chains before Dunan.

He stared stonily at the young man, "what do you want?"

Stumbling over his words Dunan said, "I know my father doesn't believe you but I know you are the Nejus. What are you doing on Jukirla?"

Kittal kept the young man standing as he tried to decide whether to let him know. There was something about the privileged young man that he couldn't put his finger on. There was an interest in the dragons and not just a passing one, "I am after knowledge. A long time ago some Suwars left Keytel to find a new home for themselves. I am now seeking them to find out what happened to them and make contact with them."

"You think they came here?"

"Yes." He eyed the young man, "you know something?"

"I confess I have been fascinated with dragons ever since I saw my first one. I have read everything we have on our history with them." Dunan puffed out his chest.

"And what did you find out?"

"Your Suwars did come here. In the histories it is recorded they came from the mountains where wild dragons had fought them off. They took a stronger stance here and trapped the dragons they found here before they could defend themselves. They were smaller then and were easily overpowered by the Suwars and their dragons. The Suwars then turned on their own as their dragons objected to the treatment of the wild ones."

"Thank you." Kittal said quietly. His hands were fists in his angst at what had happened to both the dragons and the Suwars. That was now in the past and the future was more important, "and what do you think of them?"

"They are dangerous."

"How do you know that since they are chained up all the time?"

Dunan hesitated before pointing at Kittal and saying, "just look at you."

"What about me?"

"I know your scar was from a dragon."

"That it?" Kittal challenged, "he didn't attack me. Do you know anyone else who has been hurt by one?"

Dunan, in embarrassment, bowed his head as he shook it.

"So are they dangerous? They can be if treated poorly and do you know, if their chains broke today some would look for revenge but others just want to live peacefully. I can say this because I live with them, protect them, talk to them. Have you ever tried?"

"No."

"They are not interested in man. We invaded their lands."

"That's enough." An overseer appeared and snarled, "this is our lands. Do not try to change our ways Nobody." He pulled Kittal out of the hut and shoved him to the ground. He kicked Kittal, "get up and get back to work."

"Don't touch me." Kittal snarled as he got to his feet.

"You can't order me Nobody." And the overseer shoved him back to the ground.

With a snarl Kittal leapt up and threw his chained hands over the man's head and pulled the chains tight against his throat. He needed to get away, get home and come back with reinforcements.

The man fought the chains, trying to get his fingers behind them. The other overseers ran over but it was too late for their friend. They all leapt on Kittal but he threw them off. He felt the dragons cheering in his mind. The air was pushed out of him as the overseers jumped on him again and this time he wasn't going to get up.

They dragged him up and marched him to the punishment pole and tied him to it. The head overseer turned and snarled at the workers, "get back to work."

Dunan watched the fight from the doorway of the hut. He had not expected it. The head overseer approached, "he will be punished in the morning. He can stay there and think about what he's done."

"He doesn't belong here." Dunan objected.

"Your father says otherwise. He's a troublemaker already and is where he belongs. The dragons are where they belong too."

"They deserve to be free."

"Don't let your father hear you say that." The overseer warned, "now go before he finds out you were here."

Sixteen

That was the first whipping of many. Through all the pain, suffering and escape attempts Kittal remained strong for the dragons' sake. For so long they had waited for their saviour and he wouldn't let them down no matter how weary and worn down he was.

After breaking into the mine manager's home and being left hanging on the punishment pole for two days in the rain before being whipped in front of everyone he was thrown to the floor of the crowded hut. His fellow prison miners hung back out of fear of helping him while the two overseers glared at them. One, his foot on Kittal's bloody back, remarked with a snarl, "learn from his mistakes."

With them gone Kittal tried to get up but fell back to the packed soil floor with a moan. A woman pushed her way through the half-naked filthy men. Carefully she pulled Kittal off the floor. With one of his arms over her shoulder she turned to them, "what are you staring at? He's only doing what you all dream of doing."

They silently parted to let her pass. She helped him to his straw mattress on the floor as she shouted at one of the men, "get me some clean water you fool. Come on, you know the drill." To Kittal she said as she lowered him on to his mattress, "you've got to stop antagonising them."

He hissed as she put a damp cloth on his bleeding back, "I've got to get out of here."

"I know you want to but..." She ran out of words. She loved him even though she hadn't told him and she wasn't sure how much he loved her.

They had been together ever since he had saved her from the overseer who had been eyeing her up by breaking the man's neck with his bare hands. She was one of the few women at the mine, sent because she had killed her abusive husband. She mainly fetched the men water and made food for them with their meagre rations.

"I've been here a year which is way too long. I need my bracelet back."

"Get your strength up before you try again."

A few nights later he slipped out without disturbing his lover. He put his fingers to his lips when one of the men glanced up and rolled his eyes. He had been there as long as Kittal and knew how hard the man was trying to get out. He bore everything the overseers threw at him and more. They all knew he had a special connection to the dragons although only a few believed it and only after seeing how he interacted with them.

Out under the starlit sky Kittal slipped across the yard via the shadows to the mine manager's house which sat slightly above the mine's workshops. He knew his bracelet was there, thrown in a box as if it was a piece of trash. That first day two of the beads had broken as it had landed in the box and the power within those returned to him like he had been kicked in the chest again. With it back he would be able to finally escape and get back to Keytel.

He peered through the windows till he saw the box of possessions in the man's office. With the crowbar he had borrowed from one of the workshops he levered open the window. He froze as the wood creaked in protest. There was no sound from the house so he pushed the window up further. He climbed in and with bare feet he crept across the room and reclaimed his bracelet with a sigh of relief. He felt some of the exhaustion disappear as his hand touched it. A smiled played on his cracked lips as he also spotted his knife and reached for that too.

He returned to the hut and placed the bracelet and knife in his hiding place in the rafters. In the morning he would speak to the men and the dragon he worked alongside. He slipped back into bed and wrapped his arm round his lover. She snuggled in and happily sighed. He kissed her neck and she rolled over and pouted when he didn't go any further.

Two nights later everyone was set. The men crouched around Kittal as he said, "do what you need to do but no more. They will be after me so leave them to me and the dragons."

"We want to do more than that. We've all suffered by their hand."

"Fine but stay out of my way." He said sternly.

"Good luck Kittal."

The men headed out after checking it was clear, slipping out one by one, till only his lover was left. She clung to Kittal as he tried to get her to stay. He briefly found it endearing but then found it annoying, "I can't take you with me. You are safer here."

"Why can't I come with you?"

"You wouldn't become my Nejusana." He retorted angrily.

"Oh." She stepped away from him then, "oh."

He walked out then. He didn't need a lingering farewell delaying him.

The others had scattered to their positions and now they were on their own as Kittal boldly walked across to where the dragons lay chained to the ground. The dragons watched as their guard became alert. The guard pointed his spear at him. Kittal waved his hand at the guard and the man went flying as he continued to walk towards the dragons. With the bracelet spinning at his wrist he controlled the power within it and he broke the chains of all the dragons while he walked to a dark green one. He asked, *"you ready for this?"*

"I'm going to love this bit."

Kittal climbed on to the dragon and leant over the broken, weakened wings of the dragon. Power from the bracelet passed through him and down into the wings of the dragon. The dragon lifted them and flapped them and felt the air and dust move. Carefully he rose into the air with Kittal on his back. They circled the buildings.

The overseers and guards were panicking over the fires that had suddenly started in the buildings until they saw the faltering dragon who was trying to fly with Kittal clinging to his back. Kittal had done all he could but now the dragon had to quickly learn how to fly. It dropped to the ground out of breath. Kittal dropped off and slapped his hands together. A ball of fire went soaring through the air at three guards running towards him.

One of the guards ducked out of the way and ran round, sword in hand. Kittal pulled his knife out of his waistband and threw it. The man fell backwards, a surprised look on his face with the knife in his throat. Kittal ran towards his knife, grabbed it, blood spurting in his face and grabbed the sword before carried on, charging at the overseers who were ill prepared for his attack.

He slashed one in the face and as he raised to take out another a whip wrapped round his wrist. He dropped the sword. Kittal span round with a roar and leapt on the man. The whip became slack as the man's neck was broken. He grabbed the whip and flickered it at the next man heading towards him.

The other prisoners charged in and were soon fighting their overseers and guards. Kittal turned and ran for the dragon who had taken off again. He grabbed the dragon's tail and as he rose into the air Kittal used the movement of the tail to reach the dragon's back.

Below someone had found a bow and was firing arrows at them. Kittal grunted as one struck him in the shoulder. He clung tighter to the dragon with his knees. He called out, "*do you think you can get us out of here?*"

"*I can try.*"

"*Then go, go!*" Kittal shouted as he broke the arrow in his shoulder. He held up his hand so the glowing light of bracelet lit the way through the moonless sky.

They flew through the night till they reached the coast of the mainland. They passed by Senspanta and up the coast till they found an empty cove. The dragon crash landed into the surf and Kittal fell off. The dragon picked him up out of the surf and carried him out of the way of the waves. He sniffed at the wound before settling beside Kittal to wait for him to come round....

Seventeen

Ciara couldn't help it. She put an arm around her brother and he leant into it. He finished, "I'm not sure how long we were there until I was found. The dragon had died. Once I had recovered enough to keep moving I headed to the mountains. It took me a while."

"How many of my Suwars do you need?" She looked down at her dangling feet. They sat on the edge of a cliff like they use to when they were children. She swung them.

"As many as are willing."

"I will see who will go without leaving the valley unguarded."

"Thank you." He gave her a tight smile.

"They need to be saved."

They both looked up when there was a roar. They looked to each other as Kittal said, "we need to get back to the house." He pushed himself away from the edge before getting up and helping his sister up.

Reaching the house they found Kite on the lawn and Kittal demanded, *"what has happened? Why are you not with your child?"*

"She has been taken, along with the two mountain enfants." Kite replied as she danced on her feet and claws, wanting to go and find her child.

"Canaan!"

"Sir?"

"My bow and arrows." Kittal ordered.

It wasn't long before he was in the air, riding bare back on an angry Kite. Both pairs of eyes were looking down at the ground, Kittal's almost as good as Kite's now he held all the powers of a Nejus. He could see almost every leaf as they were rustled by the wind.

He spotted movement of vegetation that a gentle breeze wouldn't be able to cause. He nudged Kite right with a knee as he put an arrow to his bowstring, his eyes not leaving the movement. There was a brief glimpse of the men in green scruffy clothing, but then they disappeared back into the undergrowth. Kittal hissed, "we've got you now."

The men below glanced up and saw the dragon with its rider and gulped nervously. While six of them carried the wiggling chained dragons the one at the back of the group paused long enough to release an arrow. The arrow pierced Kite in a soft spot where her wing joined her body. She staggered mid-flight but saved herself and Kittal.

He started to run again and catch up with the group. Looking behind he saw the dragon and rider were still following them. He saw Kite's mouth open in a roar and he felt his eardrums burst and blood dripped from his ear. He saw the number of sharp teeth which filled her mouth. He saw the large claws on her wings stretching out for him. He stumbled and fell to the ground. Turning he scrambled to his feet, leaving his bow behind. He was running for his life now.

Kittal aimed his bow at the man and he fell with a cry. His companions barely glanced round. They were heading for the rest of the group who were on horseback, holding riderless steeds, around a horse and cart. As soon as the baby dragons were on the cart they would be off. They fired up at the dragon and rider with their bows. Kittal released an arrow after setting it alight. The cart was quickly ablaze and the horse broke the reins and ran, wild eyed. No one could stop it.

Kite roared and swooped down on the now galloping horsemen. They couldn't stop the horses from going. The baby dragons were abandoned as the men went for their horses before they completely disappeared. A ball of fire exploded from her mouth. The men should have had more sense than to mess with a mother. She roared again as the fire missed the horsemen as they swerved round the blackened ground where the fireball had hit. Kittal was only just in control of her as she turned to take another go. Her maternal instincts were stronger than her role as dragon ride to her rider.

He put another arrow to his bow and aimed it at the head of the group who flopped over his horse's head causing the equine animal to swerve away from the others with a whinny of fear. The rest continued to gallop on with their bows bouncing on their backs.   Another fireball from Kite landed directly in the middle of the group killing the central rider instantly in a ball of intense heat. She was annoyed that she hadn't killed the man that had captured her newly hatched daughter. She snarled and turned, Kittal only just staying on her back as she turned at such a steep angle. He glanced behind and saw a man firing up at them, the arrows flying by. He ducked low over Kite's back as he put another arrow to his bow, she may be protected but he wasn't. Twisting round he shot the shooter dead.

Kite suddenly pulled up short as she saw something she didn't recognise heading towards her. She didn't get a chance to move and Kittal was busy with another of the enemy. He only realised there was something wrong as he found himself heading towards the ground on Kite, both wrapped in a net. He shouted, *"pull up! Pull up!"*

She crashed to the ground and rolled on to her side trapping Kittal under her. He struggled to get out from under her. Looking up he found themselves surrounded by new riders with arrows aimed at him.

He stopped struggling and glared at them from where he lay on his back in the grass with his free leg resting on her back. One of the archers said, "make a move and you die with it."

Kittal snarled and his hands became fists though there was nothing he could do. He glanced round and saw his bow lying behind the men and all his arrows snapped from Kite's impact on the ground. He breathed heavily, his chest rising and falling quickly as he grew angry with himself for not seeing that it was going to happen. He felt Kite shift and said, *"don't move Kite, just breath out."*

Kite breathed out and Kittal tried to pull his leg out from under her with no luck.

He closed his eyes and tightened his fists so he felt his nails digging into his skin. His lips began to move as he whispered a spell that he didn't need to do but it was enough to make the men nervous. One ordered, "stop that! Stop that, or we'll shoot."

Kittal continued to murmur his spell as he spoke to Kite through her mind, *"release a fireball when I say.... Now!"* As she released a fireball at her own guard Kittal slapped his hands together sending a fireball straight at the men. They dropped to the ground burnt and dead as the rest decided to flee. Kittal eyed the dead for a minute before deciding it was safe. He said, *"Kite can you get up? You are on my leg."*

"Sorry sir." Kite tried to rise. She rose just enough for Kittal to pull his leg free before she fell back to the ground on her side with a moan.

Kittal, untangled himself from the net, stood and dusted himself down. He walked round and looked at Kite with concern. Couching down he said, *"let me take a look girl."*

She moved her wing to reveal the broken shaft of the arrow. He carefully pulled it out. She hissed at the pain making him say in reply, *"ssh, I'll get this sorted. Can't lose you now."* He gave her a tight smile before concentrating on the wound. The wound began to close, growing smaller by the second. Once it was completely healed by Kittal Kite got to her feet. She looked at her chest and then at her Nejus who was looking at her sternly now. He asked, *"have you finished? Calmed down?"*

"Yes sir, I'm sorry sir."

"Let's go get the babies back to the valley." He ran across the land to where the three babies had been abandoned. He pulled the nets off them and broke the chains. Behind him Kite hissed at the wounds the chains had made on the new-born's scales. Kittal said, *"we'll get her back and then I'll sort out the wounds. Right, little ones, can you two fly?"* The two little mountain dragons nodded and jumped up and down.

"Let's head home then."

Kittal climbed back on to Kite as she gently picked up her daughter. She rose into the air along with the two little mountain dragons.

Back at the house Kittal carried the new born dragon out of the glaring evening sun. He studied the wounds made by the chains and found none of them serious. He closed his eyes to calm his beating heart before running his hands slowly over the raw bloody soft scales and healed the wounds.

Kittal went out to the worried Kite where Lupe had also joined her. He rubbed his forehead with the back of a bloody hand. He sighed and then gave his dragon a smile, *"she will recover. I'll keep her here until her scales have hardened so it can't happen again."*

"Thank you." Kite said with relief. She glanced at Lupe who looked relieved as well.

Lying in bed next to Kittal that night Lulizen felt concerned for him. He had spent most of the day with his sister and then with Kite finding her daughter and the two mountain babies. They should have still been celebrating their joining but he looked weary. She rolled on to her side to look at him as he gazed up at the ceiling of open rafters. He sighed and turned away from her. She touched his arm and he glanced over at her out of the corner of his left eye. She asked, "what are you thinking about?"

"Nothing." He replied, "there are things that we need to talk about Kittal."

"In the morning." He answered stiffly.

With the morning he led her away from the house so they could talk alone. He kept a hold of her hand as he drew her further into the green vegetation with birdsong and the buzzing of insects all around them. Coming to a small clear pool crowded by trees, which hung over the sides, he sat by the edge of the still water. Lulizen sat next to him and asked, "why couldn't you have told me about the ceremony yourself?"

He kept his eyes fixed on the clear water where the bottom of rock could be seen and fishes flittered in and out of the light which reflected on their scales. Turning away he finally said, "I felt embarrassed by it. Nothing is as barbaric as what the law of my land says must be done. I didn't want to frighten you away since I wanted you by my side." He looked at her with a faint plead in his grey eyes. She gave him a faint smile as she said, "I forgive you." She gave him a kiss.

They sat in silence for a long time until Kittal lay down, his head resting on his hands as he stared up at the blue sky. With the warm sun on him his eyes began to close and he drifted off and rolled on to his side. Lulizen looked down at him and brushed her hair off her face as she smiled. She pulled the seeds off another piece of grass as she looked around. She turned and looked at him again. She knew the scars were real but still she wanted to touch them to make sure they still were. Kittal tried to stifle his laugh as he felt her fingers on his back. He opened his eyes and took hold of her wrist, stopping her, "don't, it tickles."

"How did you get them?"

The smile he had slipped from his face and his expression became solemn. He sat up and looked across the pool as he said, "before I came to the mountains, I was on the island of Jukirla. I was injured escaping," he rubbed the puckered scar on his shoulder, "and the scars on my back were from the whippings I received at the mine where I was kept as a prisoner."

"Oh." She regretted asking.

"That is why Titan thinks he is entitled to rule now. I was away too long."

"What can I do to help?" She wanted to be useful like everyone else.

"Bear me a son so all this fighting is really worth it. If I die with no son he becomes Nejus and I don't want the Dragons to have him as their carer."

"There is no control over what sex a child is." She pointed out.

"Let us make sure there is a greater chance of it being male then." He said sounding husky. He took the hem of her dress and lifted the whole thing over her head so she sat naked before him. He removed his clothes and dived into the clear pool, which was deeper than it looked. She knelt on the edge of the pool not sure what was going on. Coming to the surface he grabbed one of her hands and pulled her closer. She resisted, "I can't swim."

"I won't let go of you."

With a reassuring smile he held out his hands and she slipped into his arms. Lulizen went under and before she could panic he pulled her to the surface. He kissed her wet lips and his arms went around her waist. He drew her under with him and she stared around as she saw the fish swim away from the pair. Kittal held her under with him, his mouth still on hers, giving her air to breath from his own lungs otherwise they would never have been able to remain under for more than a minute. He closed his eyes as he drew Lulizen closer to him, holding her tight in his hold.

As he let her go from his tight hold they surfaced where both of them gasped for breath. She stared, wide-eyed at Kittal and stammered, "what did you just do?"

He gave her a knowing smile, "just making sure that I'll have an heir."

"What do you mean?"

"This is the Pool of Heirs. A couple which bath in it are more likely to have a boy as their first child. It doesn't always work, only if both want one. Tania came about because She didn't want a boy at the time so it had no effect, nature chose a girl to be born."

"It sounds more like superstitions to me." She replied. He chuckled as he pulled her close again, putting a hand on her rounding belly.

Eighteen

Kittal wasn't there when she woke up. Heading out of the bedroom into the rest of the house she found him with a group of Suwars. They were all looking serious. Kittal had his back to Lulizen and was dressed in his flying gear, his bow in one hand. With an edge of worry she asked, "what's going on?"

He turned with a grim expression and replied, "nothing that need worry you."

"It does concern me Kittal. What would happen if you got yourself killed? Our child would grow up with no father, or teacher."

"I'm not going to get killed." He said sternly, "I'm not going to die before our son is born, I promise that. I won't die as easily as Titan will, I have the power of the dragons on my side. Go back to bed, rest."

"I'm not that delicate." She protested as she took a step closer.

Parting from the group so he could have a private word with her Kittal led Lulizen into his study where there were open books strewn everywhere. He looked into her eyes and gave her a tight smile. She asked cautiously, "where are you going?"

"Titan's castle."

"You can't." She objected and then added with determination, "I'm coming with you."

"No." He said angrily making her look frightened, "I'm not letting you get anywhere near that place. I promised to protect you and that is what I'm going to do. You stay here, understand?"

She reluctantly nodded. He continued, "you are carrying our son and to me for the duration of the pregnancy you are as fragile as a newly hatched dragon with its soft scales. I don't care if you think you could cope, I just don't want to lose either of you two because of a reckless decision." He bent down to kiss her, but she turned her head away feeling annoyed that he thought of her as being weak. He looked hurt and added, "I don't want to see you hurt by him. If he knew you existed, he would try to kill you. My valley has been attacked twice now and this can't go on. I have to stop him. He needs to learn that I am back and ruling again."

She looked at him, feeling tears welling up in her eyes, "can't I feel protective of you? I don't want to see you get hurt."

"Of course you don't, but this is what I have to do so we can bring my heir, and the others we will have, up in a peaceful time, not one of war." He took hold of her chin and lifted her head up. He gave her a tight smile, "yes?"

"Go do what has to be done," Lulizen replied reluctantly, "just be careful please."

"I will."

He left her standing in his study. She approached the doorway once he had left the room and watched him nod at the Suwars They headed out with him following behind. Outside a group of dragons were already waiting, saddled up and eager to head out over the plains towards the hills where Titan had set up home.

Kite's daughter squawked at her mother from the veranda where she had been told to remain by Kite. The little dragon flapped her wings but they were still too small to support her scaled body. She wanted to go with her mother, but knew that she had to be utterly obedient to her mother otherwise it was death, until she came of age. She dropped down on to all fours and went back into the house, to Lulizen, who she knew was carrying the person who was to be her rider and who she would be named after.

Ciara watched them go, feeling jealous of the younger generation of Suwars. She wanted to be out there with them but knew she was safer in the valley and that someone had to look after it. Kittal had already told her he feared what Titan might do if he saw that she was back with her Suwars.

With a sigh she turned away from the shrinking flying Dragons. She saw her daughter freeze at the other side of the room and then take a step backwards. Ciara stared at Leanne with a grim expression and then forcing herself to remain calm she asked, "why are you not up there?"

"I asked to be excused."

"You are not allowed to. When the Nejus or I give you an order you are expected to obey." Ciara said, fuming inside, "as a Suwar you answer to your leader or to the Nejus, you aren't allowed to back out. Do you want to be marked as a coward?"

"No." Leanne replied, shaking.

"This evening you then apologise to the Nejus, no buts about it. Now go! We'll speak more on the matter tomorrow." She turned away from her daughter.

Leanne announced, "Mother, I'm pregnant."

It was Ciara's turn to freeze and she turned back, "how? I know for one that a joining has not been arranged for you yet. How dare you go behind my back?! I should banish you, take away your spurs for this insolence. Secondly being pregnant makes no difference to going on missions, I was still doing such things when I was eight months gone. How else are you going to prove yourself as a Suwar if you don't do a mission?" Feeling weak suddenly after her outburst Ciara reached for something to support herself. Leanne ran over exclaiming, "mother?!"

"I don't want to see you for the rest of the day, get out of my sight slut, you are no daughter of mine. The Nejus will hear of this when he gets back and then you'll be for it. Go!" Ciara hissed, not even allowing her eldest to help her.

Leanne dropped her hands and hesitated, hoping that her mother would change her mind. Realising she was not wanted she left the room while trying to hold back the tears in front of her mother. She couldn't believe that she had blurted out her condition to her mother and now she had a mother who was angry with her. She brushed tears off her cheeks as she headed back to the camp. A young man came up to her as she arrived. Putting a cautious hand on her he asked, "Leanne, what's wrong?"

"Everything is wrong." She complained and looked at him, "I just told her and now she's angry with me. I didn't mean to tell her, it just came out, I'm so sorry."

"It would have been discovered at some point." He replied, attempting to console her. He wrapped his arms around her, allowing her to cry into his chest. He rubbed her back nervously. She mumbled into his chest, "I've ruined any chance of us being joined."

"We'll put our case forward together when the Nejus asks for us, agreed?"

She glanced up at him and gave him a tight smile, "yes."

"That's settled then, so don't worry for the moment." He kissed the top of her head and brushed her brown hair from her teary face where it was sticking to her cheek.

Nineteen

The group flew in silence with Kittal leading the way towards Titan's castle. As their shadows crossed over the grassland and woods birds rose up and animals looked up, young ones scattering in fear from the sight of the dragons. The group kept away from towns so that Titan could not be alerted.

When Titan's castle came into view, dark grey against the blue cloudless sky Kittal said to Kite, *"head down when we are a bit closer. I want them to see us now."*
Drawing closer the dragon turned, leaning into the turn, as she headed towards the ground. The others followed behind her, their wings spread out as they soared downwards, circling to slow down. They landed on the rocky ground on either side of the road leading to the castle.

The guards on the castle wall looked across nervously as they knew there was going to be trouble if their Nejus had shown up with Suwars. The Suwars watched as more appeared on the wall, men from Jukirla. These didn't look afraid of the dragons. They knew what to do with troublesome dragons. Kittal said to his men, "I go on foot from here. I do not expect this to be easy."

The Suwars rose into the air as Kittal marched into the courtyard. The Keytellians warily watched Kittal while the islanders were sneering at the Suwars who had all armed their bows. Kittal pulled off his gloves as he looked around at the men on the battlements. Spears and arrows were aimed at both him and his hovering Suwars. He shouted, "I am Kittal,

Nejus of Keytel. This is not your fight. Go home!" He turned and faced the castle keep, "Titan! Show yourself."

Titan watched from a window. A servant appeared and said, "your brother is here with some of his Suwars."

"I can see that. Invite him in." He didn't turn from the window, "and send in Trom."

"Yes sir."

Trom, dressed in a plain coat, trousers and boots appeared, "you asked for me?"

"Come here." Titan beckoned Trom across to the window. Trom approached and looked out. He saw the man in the courtyard and the men in the air.

"Down there is my brother. He is here to tame me. He has been gone too long and this is my country now. He may have entered peacefully but it won't remain so. They are going to fight hard. My brother is a good soldier and leader and the Suwars are equal to him. He has powers that your men know nothing of. I want him alive."

"I am aware of him. I lost a brother to him and he also destroyed a lot of property back on Jukirla. We want our revenge."

"Ha. You have failed so far. You have underestimated him."

"So we have found to our cost. Help us like we are helping you."

"Of course." Titan said with little emotion, "go now."

With the man gone Titan commented to himself, "I will win this brother and then nothing will stop me."
In the dust on the windowsill he drew the outline of a scorpion with a finger. From the outline rose a scorpion with its tail larger than its pincers. To the small deadly creature he said, *"when he arrives, get him. I want him incapable of leaving once he is here. I can't trust those men to capture him, he won't allow it."*
The scorpion scuttled down from the windowsill and across the floorboards. Titan watched with a smile on his face. His

brother had always underestimated him. He had read the same books Kittal had.

The air was becoming charged. Fighting could start at any moment but neither side wanted to make the first move. Kittal and his Suwars eyed the servant suspiciously as he nervously stepped out. The man remained in the safety of the doorway as he said, "Nejus, my master requests your presence inside."

"Tell him to step out and kneel at my feet and ask for mercy or face worst."

The servant gulped and looked upwards. Kittal followed his eyes and spotted his brother hiding. He shouted, "you are a coward Titan."

Titan opened the window and sneered, "who is in the safer position?"

Kittal snarled, "prepare to die." He pulled out his knife and threw it at the window. It clattered against the stonework. Titan laughed and then stopped. He shouted, "kill them!"

Kittal dived for the door which the servant was trying to close as five of his Suwars swung down from their dragons and followed him inside. The rest covered them by firing their arrows at the men on the battlements.

Inside Kittal jumped on the servant and with another knife slit his throat. He turned to the Suwars, "prepare yourselves. Expect the worst." He pulled out the knife and wiped the blood off it. He felt no remorse for the dead man.

Before they got far the balconies above the great staircase filled with soldiers with Trom at the head of the stairs. Kittal hissed, "no hesitating."

His Suwars already had pulled back bowstrings and as one fired arrows upwards. Kittal pulled out a curved sword from its scabbard and ran up the stairs with his Suwars.

Titan's soldiers began falling, dead and injured. Kittal found himself facing Trom. They both paused. Trom let his desire for revenge to get the better of him and charged first. He cried out, "this is for my brother."

Kittal sidestepped him and made to slash at Trom with a growl. Trom managed to defend himself but didn't see Kittal's knife thrust up, under his ribcage. Kittal pulled his knife out and Trom fell to the floor. Kittal forced his way through them and onwards. He ran through the castle's corridors followed by his Suwars. He didn't see the magical scorpion scuttle out of the way of his booted feet.

It caught hold of Kittal's boot with a small claw and slowly made its way up the boot. Reaching the top of the boot it paused making a decision on which way to go, the one that would freeze Kittal the quickest. It was almost thrown off as Kittal knocked against a wall to get out of the way of a flying arrow. It scurried down inside his boot, its tail curled up close to its body so it wouldn't be detected too soon.

Kittal didn't know of the scorpion in his boot as he led the way into the room he knew Titan had been in. He swore when he found it empty. He threw the furniture around the room in his anger. Titan had disappeared and he had found support from the Jukirlans.   He looked out of the window and five of his Suwars were lying dead in the courtyard and one dragon however most of the men on the battlements were also dead or injured. He smiled, they had fought well. He turned back to the Suwars with him, "I am ordering you to go home and reassure my sister that I will be there shortly after. I must find my brother. Take the dead with you as well."
He turned and opened the window and then whistled, placing two fingers in his mouth.

Reluctantly they climbed out of the window and jumped on to the hind leg of their dragons and scrambled up into their saddles. The last to leave looked to his Nejus, "are you sure about this sir?"

"Just go." Kittal growled. He turned and stalked back into the castle in search of his brother.

He threw doors open but found nothing apart from Titan's mistress. She screamed but that stopped when he slashed her with his sabre. He moved on until he came to the rooftop of the keep. He found Titan there and shouted, "I am Nejus. These are my lands. Send out a decree and kneel before me as your overlord."

"No."

"Your mistress is dead and so are most of your men." Titan looked shocked but quickly recovered, "no!" Kittal began to advance on his brother who chose to flee.

"Come and face me you coward." Kittal put an arrow to his bowstring and released it just as the scorpion chose to strike with its poisoned tail. The arrow which should have killed Titan hit him in the shoulder, spinning him before he fell to his knees. He staggered up and kept going.

As for the scorpion it dug its sting deep into Kittal's ankle. Through clenched teeth he hissed in the pain and frustration that his shot had missed his brother's heart. He crouched down and press hard against where he had been stung, killing the creature. He tried to move and found that his whole leg had gone numb and he dropped to his knee. He whistled and Kite appeared. She said with concern, *"I was beginning to worry. All the others have gone."*

"Grab hold of me and get me away from here. I can't move." She caught him by the shoulders and carried him away as men appeared. The Suwars appeared, having ignored his orders, and gave Kite and their Nejus covering fire as they flew away.

She placed Kittal down a mile from the castle with the Suwars landing around him. He crumpled to the ground, unable to stand on his feet. She landed beside him and asked with worry, *"what is wrong?"*

"I don't know old girl. Felt this stinging pain and that was it, couldn't move." He glanced up at Kite with worry written in his grey eyes.

He turned his attention back on himself and took his left boot off. He saw the scorpion squashed against his bare ankle, its poisoned sting piercing his skin. He took his small knife from his other boot and dug a hole round where the scorpion had stung him. Carefully he levered the small piece of cut flesh from him leaving a bleeding hole. He felt tears welling up as he did. He muttered to try and forget the tears, "Titan! Thought you got the better of me, but you never will. That damn poison is still in me, but I know how to reverse it, need to get home though." He tore a piece of his turban off and wrapped it round his swollen and bleeding ankle. He attempted to stand but found he was still under the effects of the poison that was pumping through his blood. He muttered, "I will kill that damn man next time round. It won't be me." To Kite he said, *"help me up will you. I'm still unable to move my leg, that damn Titan."*

Kite crouched low and he grabbed the saddle's stirrup. He pulled himself up. Kite helped him to get on the saddle sideways with a forearm. He smiled his thanks and remarked, *"go carefully but quickly, I haven't got much in the way of grip, this saddle wasn't made to be rode like this."* She carefully rose into the air. Kittal clung to the front of the saddle as she turned in the direction of the valley and home.

Twenty

Reaching home he ordered Canaan to make a poultice of herbs which would draw out the poison and cool down the swelling. He rapped out the list as he sat in the main room with his leg up. With it made up he told Canaan to press it against his self-inflicted wound and wrap a bandage around it to hold it in place. With that done he sat back, now able to breath easy. He closed his eyes with a sigh, not planning to do anything more for the rest of the day.

He wasn't allowed to rest though since he was Nejus and High Chieftain of the Suwars. He opened his eyes as he felt someone's presence. Across from him his sister had sat down. He sighed, "what is it?"

Ciara said to him, "Leanne needs to be disciplined."

"She is your daughter, not mine."

"No. This is more serious." She said sternly, "she disobeyed your orders and she is pregnant when she isn't joined."

"By whom?"

"I didn't ask." She replied, feeling slightly embarrassed by the question, "I just felt so angry with her for it."

"I suppose it is my turn to amend your mess. I hope it will make us even." He remarked solemnly.

"It would, yes."

"Best call her in and everyone else."

"I will." She said, not wishing to have to go through with it now but she had brought it up and Kittal was free for the moment even if injured.

Soon Leanne was standing in front of Kittal with everyone around making her feel even more ashamed than she had been feeling beforehand. She had been looking forward to having her lover's child but now she wasn't so sure. Kittal had his arms crossed in front of him and was eyeing her and the young man that was standing just behind her. There was complete silence as they were waiting for Kittal to speak, "for starters you disobeyed an order this morning, not joining myself and the other chosen Suwars on the mission. If that wasn't enough you lied to your mother, saying I had excused you when I did no such thing. You didn't even come to me to ask to be excused. In addition you have been sleeping with a man before you have been joined."

"Tania is..." She began to protest. Kittal held up a hand to silence her and he replied, "my daughter is another matter. I gave her permission. You, however, have not asked of it from your mother." He turned to look at the young man and continued, "and as for you young man you should know better." Kittal looked round all that had gathered and demanded, "who are his parents?"

Two stepped forward looking nervous, the father saying, "yes Nejus?"

"Why have you not taught your son the manners of a Suwar?"

"We did not know of this until now Nejus." The mother replied, "we brought him up properly and we are as unhappy about this as you are. He is promised to another and now that will have to be broken."

Kittal turned back to the two young adults, "you have both brought this upon yourselves."

The young man stepped forward to protest, "sir, we love each other."

Kittal eyed the man for a moment, taking him in with his mess of brown hair and hazel eyes in a long thin face before saying, "fair enough, but you both behaved wrongly, causing trouble. A child cannot be without a father. You will have to join with Leanne."

The pair turned to hug each other but Kittal hadn't finished and he warned, "don't think you are getting off this easily, both of you will receive punishments. You'll be given them tomorrow morning. Now, all of you leave, I've had enough for one day."

They bowed towards Kittal and saluted, fists pressed against chests, before shuffling out. Seeing Ciara remaining he added softly, "you too please sister. Be with your family and I'll be with mine."

She crossed over to him and placed a kiss on his head, "enjoy your evening brother."

"You too." He smiled kindly at her as she turned to leave.

Kittal's wife and daughter joined him. He put an arm round each as they curled up close against him. Tania remarked, "don't you think you are being a bit harsh on Leanne?"

Kittal looked at his daughter and gave her a tight smile, "it has to be done, otherwise there will be more who will be able to get away with it. If that happened we would lose our traditions. I can't let that happen." He sighed and added, "we should think about you joining with Canaan as well, before you become pregnant, as an example to others."

"I suppose so." She replied softly.

They looked up as Canaan appeared carrying dinner on a tray. Kittal said to his servant, "Canaan there is something we need to talk about."

"When Nejus?"

"Now, join us. You are a member of this family now in all but name."

Feeling worried Canaan sat down opposite the family making Kittal say, "come closer man, there is no reason for you to be over there since you sleep with my daughter."

Tania moved to sit with her lover as Canaan asked nervously, "what do you want to talk about?"

"Joinings, you and Tania. It is time you were joined, before a child appears. An example needs to be made. In a week's time would be good, give us enough time to prepare and then it can be done with Leanne and her man."

"That soon?! Father you can't!" Tania protested and would have continued hadn't her father not eyed her sternly. She deserved more than a quiet ceremony with another couple who were in disgrace. She wanted the splendour that came with being the Nejus' daughter. She hid the relief well as she had dreaded the thought of that brutal ancient ceremony, she had witnessed many times in her life. No girl or woman wanted it.

He said to her, "it must be done, no more objections Tania." He stood unsteadily and somehow managed to leave them for coolness of the veranda.

Outside the sun was on the verge of setting. Kittal sat down on the steps and stared out at the jungle of vegetation on the far side of the lawn. A few swallows were around, swooping up and down, taking a last chance to catch a meal before roosting for the night. He rested elbows on his knees and head in hands as he sighed. He needed to think of a suitable punishment for Leanne and her man, one that couldn't be thought of as forgiving them. He didn't want to go as far as taking their spurs because he needed as many Suwars as possible and what they had been accused of wasn't that serious. He couldn't ban them from riding either since Leanne would accept that willingly as she was pregnant.

He was still thinking as Lulizen sat by his side. She asked quietly, "what are you thinking about?"

"Punishments." He turned to look at her, "I don't know what to do. There would be an advantage for them to all the ones I that think of."

She looked thoughtful and then suggested, "split them up." He stared at her, "what do you mean?"

"Though they may be joined don't allow them to live together. Have one here and the other somewhere else and make sure they are never alone. It will make them realise if they need each other or not. It might make them concentrate on what matters at the moment, their lives and that of their families." She explained and then realised what she had just said. Living with Kittal had definitely begun to change her views on life especially as there was war on though it was hardly noticeable in the valley, "give them an experience they'll never forget."

He looked at her as he mentally worked out the finer details of what she had just said. Finally he smiled and kissed her and said, "what would have I done without you. I love you. Come to bed."

"I've learnt from the best." She teased as she got to her feet to follow him to bed.

With the morning Kittal had recovered from the scorpion's venom. Leanne and her young man were called into the study where he eyed them as they stood before him. They shifted their feet as Kittal's gaze made them uncomfortable. They looked up from their feet as Kittal spoke, "I have made a decision. Though this is a punishment take it as a chance to learn things about life as well. Leanne you are to go to the village and do some learning on how to be a woman and wife. Young man….?"

"Rolande sir."

"Rolande, you will remain here in this house. You'll be expected to help Canaan. Neither of you are to make contact with each other. You must always be with someone so you don't meet up. If somehow you end up working together you mustn't talk. You are being isolated from each other understand that." He ended solemnly as he looked at them with a stern expression, "you have done wrong, remember that."

"For how long Nejus?" Rolande asked nervously.

"Until I decide otherwise, now get out of my sight. You are to be joined in a week, but you will be split up tomorrow. There will be little celebrating on your part, understand? You are to be joined with Tania and Canaan but you won't have a night together."

"Yes Nejus." They both replied as they bowed and then left. Out on the veranda they embraced, relieved and scared at the same time. Rolande remarked, "we must not do anything to anger him. The better we behave the sooner he may forgive us."

Leanne nodded though tears ran down her face. She clung to him, not wanting to be separated from him.

Twenty-One

Before he could plan another attack on Titan's home Lulizen became his priority. Her time was drawing close and he became protective of her. He didn't want to lose his heir at such a late stage. He delayed his plans to rescue the Jukirlan dragons for her and she knew it.

The time came, two weeks early according to Lulizen's calculations. She was the only one really worried about this, no one else was, not even Kittal. He remained with her during the whole birth, though she was embarrassed by his presence, not wanting him to see her looking and feeling so terrible from pain. She leant against him on their bed, clinging tight to his hand. The midwife attending wrapped the male infant in an old blanket as it wailed. Kittal gave Lulizen a soothing mixture containing opium, which sent her to sleep.

He took his son from her and wiped blood from its face with the edge of his tunic. Ciara peered over his arm with a smile, "finally."

"Yes."

She didn't stop her brother taking the minutes old child away. He had a ritual to do. She handed him the red linen blanket, which had always been used for all the Nejus' children. It had an embroidered edge and was a little worn in places. She murmured as he walked away, "a perfectly healthy son Kittal. I am so pleased for you."

He smiled back at her and said with a hint of disbelief, "my heir, and my son."

He carried the baby up to the carved out room in the cliff. He dipped his son in the font and carefully washed the remains of the birth into the world off his wrinkled skin. The baby howled at the feel of cold water on its skin. Kittal hushed it and wrapped it in the soft red blanket. He knelt before the statue of the Dragon God and held his son up, the blanket unwrapping itself. To the statue he said, *"recognise this boy, my son, as my heir to my title as Nejus of the Dragons and Keytel. Take care of him and teach him if I should die before I have taught him all he should know. Know that all will be taught to him by father and mother as he was created through the love of both."*

"Name him." Came the disembodied reply.

"His name is to be and will be forever Ozanus, son of Lord Kittal."

"An acceptable name, his Dragon is to be known as Ozi."

"Thank you." Kittal bowed his head and drew his son to his chest. He stood and burnt the old now bloody blanket with a red-hot glowing hand, it was of no use now. He headed back to the house.

Lulizen only slept for a few minutes. She was unable to do so any longer as she was worried for her child. She didn't know what sex it was or whether it was alive. She opened her eyes and looked around. She saw Ciara and asked, "where is it? It is alive isn't it? I'm sure it was two weeks early."

Ciara crossed to her and replied kindly, "Kittal has him, your son. He is alive don't worry. He is a strong child."

"What is Kittal doing with him?" Lulizen asked with fear.

"Telling the Dragon Lord of his next man and naming him."

"He hasn't asked me." Lulizen said, not sure how she should feel about that.

Ciara saw the confused expression and said, "he will chose a suitable name."

"I wanted to give my child a name."

"You can. What he'll be named now is his official one. I'm sure something can be added as well if you want. This name is the one that will also be given to your son's dragon. Don't fear. Rest; sleep. Kittal will return soon."
Lulizen let sleep take over her.

Ciara stood on the veranda as she waited for her brother to return. Seeing him approach she smiled and remarked, "what are we going to do with you?"
He looked up from looking at his child and smiled, feeling pleased with himself. He replied, "this is Ozanus and you can't do anything about me."
Ciara sighed and then looked at the child sleeping in his father's arms though the child must be getting hungry. She said, "you give him to me, you have a cradle to move."
　"Won't take long."
　"Quietly though, Lulizen is asleep." Ciara said sternly.

　Lulizen was startled awake by wailing. She sat up trying to work out where the sounds were coming from. She saw Tania slip out of the room. Lying next to her was Kittal, curled up. His head was at the far end with one arm hanging over the end of the bed. She sorted out the twisted tunic top that she had borrowed from Kittal. She slipped off the bed and padded round to the end of the bed. She stared at the cradle, surprised by the sight, having never seen it before. Dragons were carved into the aged cherry wood, she saw her wailing child wrapped in a red blanket. Kittal's hand hung into the cradle, narrowly being missed by the boy's kicking legs, which had escaped from the folds of the blanket.
　She took the child from the cradle and held it close to her, feeling motherly though she wasn't sure what she should do. Ciara heard from outside and appeared at the door, along with the village midwife. The midwife asked, "want some help?"
　"Please."

The woman approached and directed Lulizen to sit on a chair in the room. She instructed Lulizen on how to get the baby breast feeding and watched over it. Both glanced up as there was movement from the bed. It was only Kittal turning on the bed, sleeping still though the howling baby should have woken him up. Ciara smiled and remarked, "to think you should be the one who is tired and not him. You have done so much more than him today."

"Leave him be." Lulizen replied softly, "what has he been named?"

"He is Ozanus."

"Thank you." She smiled down at her baby boy.

Twenty-Two

There was a festive atmosphere within the Suwars camp though it should have been sober. Most of the Suwars were saddling up their dragons and checking their bows and swords. It had been a long time since they'd all been off to war and the younger Suwars were eager and nervous. The village had also come out to see them off. Children ran through the group while the adults helped the Suwars or talked to those not going.

As Kittal and Lulizen appeared everyone became quiet. All of them knew it was going to be a dangerous rescue mission led by their Nejus. All had been horrified at what Kittal had told them of chained and enslaved dragons on Jukirla. They stepped away from their dragons and assembled before their Nejus and Nejusana.

Lulizen, dressed in her robes with Ozanus in her arms was taken aback when the first Suwar knelt on one knee at her feet. She looked to Kittal who was dressed in his riding attire. He smiled warmly at her, "he is after your blessing. You have brought us luck having given birth to my heir." She nodded and looked back at the knelt Suwar. She placed a hand on the man's turbaned head. He quietly said, "Nejusana." And got up. Another took his place.

Soon they were all mounted on their dragons waiting for Kittal. Lulizen fought the tears. She had already raged at him in private which had become pleading not to go. He pulled her and his heir close to him and gave her a hard kiss.

He stepped back and lifted her chin so her eyes looked into his. He murmured, "be brave. I'll be back soon."

She turned her head to hide the welling tears. She didn't want to be left with a days old child and the possibility of losing her husband in a country that she barely understood.

She was glad that Ciara appeared by her side as Kittal mounted Kite. With her free hand she reached for Ciara's as Kite rose into the air. Ciara said, "he'll be fine. This is what he was raised to do."

The other Suwars followed as friends and family left behind called out their love and wished them luck. The villagers cheered and waved. Kittal raised a gloved hand in acknowledgement before with a nudge of a knee he led his Suwars eastwards towards the coast.

They flew for two days and ended the journey on the hills behind Senspanta. Fires were lit and Suwars gathered round them with their dragons. They would be sleeping with them tonight. Around Kittal's fire was Ciara's lieutenants all leaning over a map of Jukirla Kittal had ordered from Linyee. Rocks held the map down in each corner. He remarked, "they are going to see us coming and probably already know we are so be prepared for a fight. The dragons aren't going to be able to fly straight away so we'll need to protect them. I'm going to need two of your best men to protect me. I don't know what will happen to me once I break their chains and heal them all. We will also need to take the Governor's House." The Governor had to be dealt with for what he had done to Kittal. There was no way he was going to let the man live.

"Is there anywhere safe to land if we need to?"

"Here might be the best place." He pointed at the Smythman's estate which he had marked on the map from memory, "we will find people I know there. Any other questions? No, well good night. I must meditate."

"Sir." They saluted and left.

Kite curled around Kittal once the Suwars left his fire. She asked, *"what will happen tomorrow?"*

"Anything could happen."

"Are we really going to free them all?"

"We are."

She snorted in her satisfaction and allowed Kittal to meditate and centre himself ready for the next day.

They were all up early the next morning. The dragons stretched their wings in the early morning light. Many of the Suwars were on the edge of the ridge line looking to the horizon seeing if they could see the island behind the morning clouds. Kittal joined them and someone tentatively asked, "how long were you there sir?"

"About a year and a half in the end. They have been waiting a long time for this moment. We should all consider ourselves privileged to be the ones freeing them. Let us go. We will use the clouds as cover." Kittal walked away as he finished wrapping his turban round his face and pulled on his dragon hide gloves.

Many had never seen the sea and couldn't resist urging their dragons down to the waves to get closer to the water. They surprised an early morning fishing boat. The fishermen had never seen the like, men and women riding dragons. They leant over the side of their boat as the dragons flew past with whoops from their riders and re-joined the rest flying high above them.

As the coastline of Jukirla appeared Kittal split away with two riders as the rest split into three groups. One went towards Jukir where with roars the dragons breathed fire over the old town as the population ran for cover. Their riders fired arrows down on anyone who stayed too long on the street.

Up at the Governor's House Monzanin couldn't believe what he was seeing. A message had been sent from

Senspanta but he had scoffed at it. He shouted at the troop of soldiers guarding his home, "do not let them near this place!" Half of the men looked like they wanted to run away and were only waiting for their Governor's back to be turned.

Another group of Suwars headed for the mines where the riders found themselves being attacked by the mine guards. Several fell until others got on the ground and the hand-to-hand fighting began. The prisoners ran to the safety of the mine entrance where a dragon was filling it and protecting them with its body. It knew what was happening and felt enough comradeship to its fellow prisoners to help protect them the best it could.

High about them all was Kittal and his two Suwars. He took a deep breath. This was the scariest thing he had ever done as he didn't know what was going to happen to either him or the dragons. He stood up in his saddle and visualised the chains round the dragons on the island along with the chain netting down in the harbour. His eyes were closed as he held the visualised chains in his hand and began to pull them.

Below them the chains on the dragons began to stretch and then the links began to break. With their new freedom they stretched their limbs and flexed their wings. They snapped their jaws and tested their voices. Anyone who came too close got a nasty surprise as the dragons revealed their teeth and took a deadly bite out of a few of their gaolers.

Above them Kittal resisted the urge to sink into his saddle. Breaking all the chains had taken more out of him then he had thought. Now he had to give them the strength to leave or overpower their slavers. He held out his hands, face down, fingers spread. He began to glow with a healing aura which spread out from his fingers in waves that then spread across the island.

Gradually the dragons' sores and wounds healed. Their wing muscles grew stronger and some began to test them. All over the island dragons rose cautiously into the air and fell to earth with a thump. Nets were thrown over them to try and keep them on the ground but they were easily broken. In the sea the dragons leapt out of the water and crushed the boats they were previously chained to, sinking them and the crews creating a floating trail of debris and blood and bodies. Sharks circled warily waiting for the sea dragons to leave.

The dragons on the land found themselves being protected by the Suwars who flew in low and took out anyone trying to restrict the escape of the Jukirlan dragons. Soon they were in the air and acting like young dragons swooping and spinning and twisting in the air; even the very oldest.

Kittal's eyes rolled into the back of his head as he fell off Kite and began falling through the air. Kite dived for him closely followed by the two Suwars. She grabbed him with the claws of one wing. She allowed the two Suwars to lead her down to the Smythson estate clearing where she landed with them.

As one of the Suwars went to Kittal the other pulled his sword out as Bonn approached, armed himself. The Suwar shouted a warning, "stay back."

"Who are you?" Bonn demanded.

The other Suwar called out, "he's coming round but we need a drink for him." He unwrapped his Nejus' turban.

The first Suwar and Bonn looked over. The armed Suwar unwrapped his turban revealing a beard face and sharply said to Bonn, "you heard him."

"Is that Kittal?" Bonn pointed with his sword.

"You have no right to address him by his name. Get him a drink." The bearded Suwar growled.

Bonn reluctantly went for a bottle of wine and returned with it with Katrine carrying a jug of water and several clay cups. She puffed out her chest, no man was going to intimidate her.

The bearded Suwar glared at her. Behind them Kittal said weakly, "it's all right Da'ud. They aren't going to kill me."

"Sir?" Da'ud turned.

"Let them through." Kittal ordered.

Katrine took the wine from her husband and then pushed past with one eye on the three dragons. She crouched at Kittal's side and mixed the wine with the water. She poured a cupful and held it out to him. With a tight smile he accepted it.

From beside Da'ud Bonn demanded, "did you do this? Who are you really? What am I supposed to do with no dragons?"

"I warned your Governor and he did not believe me. I am ruler of Keytel and protector of dragons, *all* dragons. I have freed all the dragons enslaved on this island." Kittal leant heavily on Kite as he got to his feet. He handed back the empty cup, "thank you. I must go to Jukita now and see Monzanin."

"What are you going to do?" Bonn asked with fear.

"This island will be mine." Kittal remarked sternly with narrowed eyes as he pulled himself back into his saddle with Kite's help.

Bonn and Katrine stepped back as the three dragons rose into the air. As Kittal and his Suwars flew up over the trees the couple stood in silence until Katrine asked, "did that really happen or is it all a dream?"

"It's not a dream. Our island has just been conquered by …." Bonn realised that his homeland had been too easily taken by a man who was more than just a man and who had clearly been underestimated by Monzanin.

"A mad man?"

They glanced at each other as Bonn didn't answer his wife.

"If we don't have our dragons anymore, how are we to move out wood? What about compensation? He can't just free them and not give us something in return."

"We'll have to wait and see."

Kittal flew over the island gripping tight to Kite as he felt he might still come off. He was relieved to reach the Governor's House and slip out of the saddle to the ground with Da'ud. He was greeted by one of the older Suwars.

"Hamin, where is he?"

"Under guard in his audience chamber sir."

Kittal marched into the building with his hand on his sword. The doors were swung open before he had to slow down. Before him, on the floor, was the Governor of Jukirla, arms tied behind his back. Two Suwars stood either side of him. Looking up Monzanin was shocked, "you!"

"I did warn you. Now this land is under my protection."

"You can't."

"I can and I did." Kittal snarled, "take him down to his own cells." He went and sat in the Governor's chair.

He took a moment to look round the room with its portraits of the numerous Governors and gold gilt. Kittal rolled his eyes at the extravagance of it all. Thankfully he wasn't going to live with it. He would be putting one of the Suwars in charge of Jukirla. He looked across the room as Hamin approached, "what's happening out there?"

"Half of the town is burnt down and the mines will be out of action for a while."

"And the dragons?"

"Ours are talking with them."

"Good, good."

"Sir? Are you alright?" Hamin frowned.

Kittal had put a hand to his head and had closed his eyes. He waved his free hand, "I'll be fine. Organise getting everyone who lives in what is left of this city up here for the morning."

The population of Jukir whispered amongst themselves as the council stepped into the courtyard of the Governor's House. Kittal's Suwars stood round the edge of the courtyard ready for anything that might happen. In the centre of the courtyard on an improvised platform was Kittal, sword in hand, and Hamin. Knelt between them was their Governor, head down. The front of the crowd craned their necks trying to work out what was going on and passing on every little thing that happened to those further back.

Perched on the Governor's House were three dragons, the roof creaking under their weight. Kite was in the middle.

To her left was Hamin's ride, a dusky red dragon. To her right was the new leader of the Jukirlan dragons who had chosen to stay, four sets of claws digging into the tiles. Some of the wounds had healed as scars and there were new ones where he had fought off two of his competitors.

Not all of the dragons had chosen to remain. Many of the younger ones had left to explore the world and find other dragon tribes or to create a new one. They had gone with Kittal's blessing.

With the council before him Kittal spoke, "two years ago I came to this island to find dragons. I found them enslaved. I gave your Governor a chance to free them. Instead, he sent me to your mines, hoping I would die. I am now back. I have freed the dragons and claimed this land. These lands and the dragons that dwell here are now under my protection. If any harm is done to them I will be seeking justice. In turn, any harm they cause I will ensure you also find justice." He paused to allow the message to be passed back through the crowds. A minute later he carried on, "I now seek justice for the enslavement of the dragons and myself. Your Governor is no more."

He turned and before anyone could object he swung his sword and took the Governor's head off. The head rolled to the feet of the council, its mouth opening and closing. The council gasped and took a step backwards as their eyes followed the trail of blood back to the Governor's slumped headless body and then to Kittal, afraid of what he would do next.

The Governor's family let out a wail and the women collapsed against each other. Dunan cried out, "no!"
He made to run towards his father but Suwars stepped in and held him back. He fought their firm grip and glared at the man who had just killed his father; to think at one point he had been in awe of the man. Now he saw the man for who he was. He was more dangerous than the dragons he said he watched over.

Kittal turned and scowled at Dunan and the young man froze to the spot. Satisfied that Dunan was now behaving he turned back to the audience and declared, "I leave in my place Commander Hamin."
A title had been quickly made up the night before so that the council would accept him.

Hamin stepped forward to be acknowledged. He received a wary silence. Kittal didn't care. He had thrown a lot at them since stepping into the Governor's House. Jukirla would soon get use to their new governor. Hamin frowned, unsure how to react. Seeing it Kittal demanded with a shout, "bow before my representative on this island."
Everyone bowed in fear of what he might do if they didn't.

"Hmpfh. Council, come with me." Kittal stepped down from the platform and was about to return to the house when he felt Dunan still glaring at him. He crossed to the family group and studied the angry young man.

Dunan stood tense, hands as fists, in the hands of the Suwars. He broke away from the Suwars and stepped up to his father's murder and demanded, "why?!"

"Because I can." Kittal answered without emotion, "I warned him and he did not listen."
Dunan went to hit the man but Kittal grabbed his wrist and then the young man's chin and tilted his head, "now, you listen to me boy. I now rule this island and if I hear that you have been misbehaving then you can go the same way as your father."
Dunan's mother gasped and reached for her son.
Dunan yanked his head out of Kittal's hand, "I thought you were a man of fairness."

"And I am. You are free as long as you behave." Kittal responded and walked away. He didn't care how Dunan felt. He didn't know the young man apart from one conversation two years ago and he had come across foolish and idealistic then and he did still. He would soon see this was a different world now and everything done had a reason that the Nejus felt no need to justify to a young man who was far below him.

The council glanced at each other before cautiously following Kittal and Hamin into the house.

Twenty-Three

Hanging around on the top of a valley side was not Rolande's idea of fun but he had been set the task so had to do it. His dragon dozed, lying on its side with its side rising and falling softly. He glanced at him and sighed before wandering over to the edge and looking down into the greenery, which shrouded the entrance to the valley. He could see the wind blowing the trees about. There appeared to be a pattern to it, the vegetation beginning to move ahead and fading away behind. He stared down at it puzzling over it. What was he to do? He guessed he should go and report it.

As he headed over to his dragon he heard a shout from the air. Looking up he saw Diego waving from Joli, "thought you might want some company."

"Err…. Yeah, thanks. Come on down." He beckoned the two down, glad to finally have someone to talk to since his dragon was a quiet one. He would also be able to get a second opinion on what he had seen. He crossed over to Diego as Joli landed and exclaimed, "am I glad to see you. Nothing is really happening though I want to ask you something, show you something."

"Give me a moment then." Diego replied as he threw his crutch down before slipping off Joli. Rolande helped his friend up and handed the crutch over as Diego asked, "what did you want to show me?"

"This way." Rolande said, gesturing towards the edge. Diego followed him over and peered over the edge. He looked up at Rolande, "what did you see?"

"This sounds crazy…."

"Maybe not." Diego said encouragingly.

"Well the way the wind was blowing through the shrubs below didn't look right, it was as if someone or thing was moving through them." He looked at his friend and saw Diego's eyes widen. Diego said, "visitors, best fly down, get a closer look. I'll hang here, you go."

"Right, be back shortly." Rolande replied already heading over to wake his dragon up. He had sensed worry coming from Diego and had begun to worry himself.

The dragon flew down, low over the vegetation, stirring it up as much as the visitors underneath. Rolande kept his eyes constantly on the greenery, attempting to catch sight of whoever was down there. Through a gap in the vegetation he was sure he had caught sight of green clothing. Thinking it was better to be prepared for an attack he ordered his dragon to get straight to the Nejus' house.

Ciara came out of the house hoping that it was Kittal finally coming back, but was disappointed to see that it was Rolande. Still not happy with him, though he was her son-in-law, she sneered, "what do you want?"

"Is the Nejus back yet?" He asked as he slipped from his saddle and gave her a brief bow.

"Why?"

"We have visitors, and they don't look friendly."

Ciara's eyes widened and then realising that he wasn't at his set post she demanded, "why are you not at your post?"

"Diego is there. Please believe me, I speak the truth."

She felt sure he was speaking the truth but didn't want to believe it. Reluctantly she said, "alright, go fetch the village and tell them to prepare for an invasion."

Rolande headed back to his dragon while Ciara ran back into the house. She knew that if Kittal had been there he would make sure that both Tania and Lulizen were safe with Ozanus and Kite's daughter. She headed in, planning to put such belief into action.

Lulizen was inside getting Ozanus to sleep and was smiling softly at her son. Hearing Ciara's footsteps she looked up and saw the worried expression. She stood, setting Ozanus off crying. With worry in her voice she asked, "what's wrong? It's not Kittal is it?"

"We think Titan might be coming. I've got to hide you and Tania with your son and Ozi." She muttered to herself, "where are you Kittal? You need to get back" Then added aloud, "I'll find Tania." She headed off without a backward glance.

"Ciara?"

Ciara turned and Lulizen asked, "where exactly am I going to be hiding?"

"Give me a moment while I get Tania. Stay here." She held a hand up and then hurried off.

Returning, Tania was determined not to just sit with Lulizen and her half-brother and not know what was happening outside. She carried the small dragon who was flapping its wings and feeling anxious from being away from her mother. Tania exclaimed, "I'm fighting with you Ciara."

"No." Ciara turned on the younger woman for the third time, "you are important to Kittal and Canaan. You must help Lulizen with Ozi or she might try to get back to her mother."

"I'm sure Lulizen can look after her." Tania turned to Lulizen, "you would, wouldn't you?" She looked pleadingly at Lulizen.

"Well….?"

"Tania, no!" Ciara said angrily, "Not this time. If your uncle got hold of you, you would be in serious trouble." She eyed Tania sternly. Tania backed down reluctantly though she was already planning to join in the fighting. With some relief Ciara asked, "have we finished? I would like to get you hidden quickly so I can organise the Suwars and prepare them."

"We've finished Ciara, but what about Canaan and father?"

"Kittal, I have no real idea about, but let's hope he returns in time." She was very worried, not at all sure how he was doing on Jukirla.

Having been left well hidden from all by Ciara Lulizen planned to stay until someone came to fetch her out. She remained in the corner of the green bathed cave she had settled in holding little Ozanus and wishing that Kittal was there. Ozi lay close to Lulizen using her as a substitute mother for the time being until her real mother came back. Lulizen glanced over at Tania who stood by the mouth of the cave.

Looking at Lulizen Tania felt guilty about leaving her stepmother hidden with two young children, human and dragon; and unguarded at that. She turned away to build up her courage. She wanted to be out there fighting alongside Canaan. Though Ciara was in charge while her father was freeing the dragons of Jukirla Tania wanted to be out there. She felt that it was her right as Kittal's daughter to be leading the defence while Ozanus was not old enough to do so.

She turned back to look at Lulizen and coughed to get the woman's attention. Lulizen looked up and said with worry, "you are going to go aren't you?"

"I'm sorry Lulizen." Tania crossed to Lulizen and crouched down, "I've got to. I don't like sitting around not knowing."

"I understand. If I was like you I would be wanting to fight as well…" She sighed, "… but I'm not especially now that I have Ozanus. Leave me your knife for protection and go." She gave Tania a tight smile. Tania looked relieved as she undid the knife's sheath from her belt and handed it over. She placed it next to Lulizen as she said, "thank you Lulizen, I won't forget this." She gave Lulizen a smile before hurrying out of the cave to the house where everyone was gathering.

She found both men and women were lined up on the lawn in dragon hide armour and armed with bows and swords. The Suwars hung in the air and all were nervous. Ciara stood in the middle of all of them, an arrow on her bow and with gritted teeth. Having got her own bow Tania had slipped in at the back. While in the house she had buckled on her sword for when it came to hand-to-hand combat. She glanced round the large group to see if she could spot Canaan. She couldn't see him since he was on the far right while she was on the left side. Everyone's eyes were on the vegetation round the edge of the lawn, watching for movement that wasn't wind.

The people on the right tensed as they saw and heard the shrubs rustling and then stop. None of them had a chance to relax as arrows began to spit out from the shrubs and straight towards them.

Above them the Suwars returned fire with their own arrows. There were yelps as some found their mark. Excited by the thrill of a fight some of the wilder dragons flew down and reached for hidden enemy with their hind claws.

On the ground the formation was changing to face the invaders. Though a few were beginning to panic Ciara was managing to keep everyone calm and controlled with the chanting of Suwar war cries. They adopted one and soon everyone was chanting, beginning to feel sure that they would win and were unbeatable. A dragon was hit with several extra long thick shafted narrow-headed arrows and fell towards the ground with no control in its death spin. It crashed down on the house, ripping a hole through the roof where its wings got caught up and torn. It didn't matter though for it was dead and its rider barely alive.

Fighters from the village began to fall, dead or injured as they didn't have the dragonhide armour of the Suwars. Tania whispered up a defence spell, which she hoped would protect her and Canaan. Canaan saw her from across the lawn and froze, confusion on his face as he tried to work out whether he should be angry or not. Tania cried out in fear as she saw him drop injured. She began to run towards him but another dragon fell from the sky, blocking her view. She stared at the dragon and exclaimed, "Tyke!"

The horned dragon didn't react. The one eye she could see glazed over and there was one final limp effort to get up.

Finally realising how terrible the fighting was Tania froze to the spot, terrified and wishing she had obeyed Ciara and remained with Lulizen. It was all a lot worse than she thought it would be. It was nothing like the stories she had been told.

Worried for Canaan she sat down leaning against Tyke's body and began to cry. She realised at that moment that she wasn't as strong in heart as she thought she was. She hugged her knees, rocking back and forth, wanting to be anywhere but the massacre, which it was so obviously turning into.

Ciara, jumped over Tyke's ruined neck to take some shelter behind the body to catch her breath. Both women stared at each other. Ciara stared at the guilty looking Tania as she said, "you shouldn't be here."

"I'm sorry, I thought I would be fine."

"Now you are here you may as well get back into the fighting. I'm guessing you are using a spell for protection?" She eyed Tania and the younger woman nodded. Ciara continued, "right! Get out there then. We need you now." Just as she finished there was a roar as another dragon was taken out by several arrows. They both looked up and then scampered as they saw the Dragon heading towards them.

Ciara stumbled over a body and found herself looking at an islander as she attempted to get to her feet. The man leered at her with a smile of dirty irregular teeth, sword in hand. She found herself unable to move as she sensed more men gathering around her. Recovering, she swept round, her sword temporarily keeping them at bay. The first laughed but stopped when her sword hindered his forward attack. She swung round as out of the corner of her eye she saw another sword coming her way.

Her right side was unprotected and she cried out as she felt a spear get jabbed into it. She turned and hit the spear's owner with her sword, cutting his face. Another took advantage of her being distracted and swung his sword at her. She yelled out but moved too slowly to stop all of the jabs.

Seeing she was going down many of the men moved on leaving one to deal the death stroke. She fell to the ground as the last sword caught the back of her legs and then stabbed it down through her ribcage. The Jukirlan made to move on but was thrown forward as Roland's arrow went through his neck from behind.

Hearing footsteps from close by Tania turned with her sword in hand and found herself facing her uncle. He looked mildly surprised himself but then smiled warmly at her, "he has looked after you well daughter."

"Daughter?" she didn't understand and then reacted by saying, "I'm not yours, I'm Kittal's, Lord of Keytel."

"So he has made you think."

She tried to move away so as not to hear any more lies from him. She kept her eyes on him, watching him so he didn't get too close. She said, "don't get any closer, I can fight."

"I'm sure you can." Titan smiled. He reached out and she backed away but fell backwards over a body. Her sword fell from her hand. She looked round afraid now that she was unarmed. She could see her sword but couldn't reach out for it without alerting Titan. She turned and looked up at him with her eyes wide with fear. He smiled at her again as he said, "there's nothing to fear, we have a lot of catching up to do. Are you joined? Do you have any children?" He reached down to help her up.

Tania shuffled away as she said with a shake in her voice, "don't take a step closer." She glanced behind and saw her sword nearby. She reached out, stretching out her fingers to get at it. A foot pressed itself against her wrist. With fear she looked up and saw that it was Titan. She saw the smile for a moment longer and then it vanished as he remarked, "so you won't come easily then? That is a shame. I'll have to do it the hard way then." He sighed and sadly shook his head.

Now that she couldn't go anywhere, especially as she had frozen in her fear, he reached down and exchanged foot for hand. He pulled her up roughly and held tight to her wrist. He gave a sharp whistle and someone ran across the ruined lawn and saluted. Titan ordered, "tie her up and prepare to leave. It's obvious that my dear brother isn't here." He ended with a sneer and then sternly added, "sound the retreat, I have what I wanted even if it's not my brother which I would have loved so much more." He basically threw Tania into the man's arms and then stalked away, having no care as he walked over bodies from both sides. He was sure his brother would appear soon enough at his castle.

Twenty-Four

Kittal had a bad feeling all night and hadn't been able to sleep. He felt sure Titan was planning something. He had walked the Governor's House, impatiently waiting for the first light of dawn. With it he woke Hamin, "I have to go. I'm taking Da'ud and Matheu with me."

"Sir?" Hamin struggled to understand what his Nejus was saying as he sat up in his bed.

"You know what you need to do for now. You are in charge and you have the Suwars so use them if there is any trouble."

"Sir." Hamin saluted. He was still getting use to the honour that had been bestowed upon him.

"I will send your family to you. Make me and Ciara proud." Kittal turned and walked out.

The three dragons were pushed to fly hard and fast by Kittal. He was determined to get home to the valley within the day where he felt sure something was or had happened while he had been gone.

He could only stare as they approached his house and lawn. Cautiously, since she was attempting not to land on anyone that could still be alive, Kite landed. Kittal slid out of his saddle as he continued to stare around. Gingerly he began to move through the bodies, looking for anyone he could recognise. He wanted to shout to let everyone alive know he was back but feared that Titan and his island fighters may still be about, preparing to shoot him down. He passed by someone trapped under the body of a dead dragon who moaned. Kittal bent down to investigate and was surprised to find a very young man who was only just stepping out of childhood. He looked familiar and tentatively asked, "Arno?"

"Sir?"

Kittal pulled the boy out from under the dragon as he demanded, "what are you doing here? Does your father know you are here?"

"I joined the men Titan recruited. I wanted to see your home and the dragons." Arno replied.

"Are you hurt?"

"My leg."

"We'll take care of you. Let's get you into the house." Kittal bent and helped the boy up and into his arms.

"A dragon fell on the house."

"I saw. It's only the main room. We will survive." Kittal carried Arno into his home.

He put the young man down on a chair still upright on the veranda. Arno remained quiet as he watched the man turn and survey the lawn.

Looking out Kittal realised he was going to need help and wondered where the survivors were, if there were any. He wanted to go and find Tania, Ciara and Lulizen but he restrained himself, he was needed more on the battlefield. To Arno he said, "rest, I'll be back shortly with something to ease the pain. You should never have been involved in this. It is only between myself and my brother, nobody else. You are an innocence."

"I didn't kill anyone." Arno said.

"Good."

"Will I be able to go home?" Arno asked.

"Yes though you'll find it different now. It is now under my protection and the dragons are all free."

"I knew you would do it." Arno grinned.

"I must go."

He heard someone shout and turned to see who it was. A group of Suwars, many of them looking like the younger ones, ran up with Rolande in the lead shouting, "Nejus, you have returned."

"Rolande? Are you the only ones left?"

"We think so sir." Rolande replied as he reached Kittal, "except for the ones at camp with their children or who are pregnant."

"This is good, for the time being that is."

"It is?" Rolande looked surprised.

"Yes." Kittal waited a moment for the last of them to reach him, "I need you to start going through this lot…." He waved a hand over his destroyed lawn, "….. Find all that are still alive and get them off the lawn. I'll have to burn the dead, there are too many to bury."

"Nejus?" Rolande said nervously.

Kittal turned to look at the young man, "yes?"

"Our leader is dead, I saw her die…." His voice failed before he managed to finish his sentence. He gulped back tears, not believing that he was on the verge of tears as he did. The shock of seeing the death was finally catching up with him.

Shocked himself Kittal reached out to one of the veranda's vertical beams for support. It wasn't enough and he sank on to the top step. He asked in a quiet voice of shock, "revenge?"

Rolande nodded his head, "killed the man myself."

"Thank you." Kittal said with some relief. Though he was still in shock he stood, shaking it off for the time being, "right, can you do as I said. No discrimination, injured from both sides, they should never have been involved and it's not their fault they were. Do you understand?" He eyed Rolande sternly; "I'm leaving you in charge for the time being. Does Leanne live?"

"She is safe sir."

"Good. Now get on with it."

They saluted Kittal before starting to search for any injured.

He left them to it as he returned to Kite. He had to find his wife and sons. He climbed back on to Kite as he said, *"we are going to have to burn all the dead as there are too many to bury."*

"Tyke is in there."

"And Lupe?"

"I cannot see him."

"Good. We must find our families."

She nodded as she rose into the air. Once up there she began to growl in such a low tone that Kittal could only just hear it. He could feel her chest vibrate from the rumbling sound she was making deep within her. Shaping his hands around his mouth to amplify his voice he shouted, "Lulizen! Tania!"

Hearing the sound Lulizen became alert. Beside her Ozi was also alert and moving towards the front of the cave. Carefully Lulizen stood, glancing at the sleeping Ozanus. She crept to the front and peered out. At her feet Ozi let out an excited squawk. Lulizen remarked to herself, "must be Kite or Lupe. Kittal must be with whoever it is."

She looked to the sky and saw a dragon with a rider on its back, looking so like part of the grey dragon. She didn't call out just in case it was someone who was trying to trick her into revealing her hiding place. Ozi squawked again excitedly and Lulizen said to the little dragon, "sssh, don't it could be a trick."

She glanced up and saw the dragon drawing closer. She stared at the rider trying to work out whether it was Kittal or not.

She realised she was going to have to take a chance and shouted up, "Kittal! Here!"

She saw the rider's head turn and guide the dragon towards her. She held her breath from fear. There was a reply shout, "call out again Lulizen or reveal yourself! I can't see you yet!"

"Kittal, please!" She shouted with a plea in her voice.

Hearing it Kittal said to Kite, *"quick, something is wrong."* Fearing it could be Ozi Kite sped up and only just slowed down enough to land and not go straight into the tree opposite her.

Seeing it was truly Kittal Lulizen stumbled down the worn steps and ran across to him exclaiming, "Kittal, you are alive."

He held her tight, thanking his Gods for keeping her safe. Ozi had followed Lulizen out of the cave and waved her wings about as she tottered over to Kite. Kite gave her daughter a gentle knock with her snout, reassuring the little one. She snorted with pleasure as Ozi squeaked excitedly. Kittal glanced over with a smile at hearing the snort and commented to Lulizen, "she's as pleased as I am. Where is Ozanus and Tania though?"

"Tania went out to fight." She replied nervously. She felt him tense and added, "what's wrong? Is she missing? It's my fault, I didn't try to stop her."

"It's not your fault, you wouldn't have been able too; she's too head strong and too much her own person. Lets get Ozanus and then get back to the house. I'm going to need your help looking after the injured." He let go of her and headed into the cave to get little Ozanus. Once out he held Ozi while Lulizen held their son, pressing him securely into Kittal's body as Kite rose into the sky to go back to the house.

Reaching the battlefield Lulizen hid Ozanus' head in her breast before he could see the bodies strewn across the ruined lawn and then be haunted by it. To Kittal she said, "I'm sorry but I can't stay here, not with Ozanus anyway."

He turned with a concerned look, "are you sure?"

She nodded, "I don't want it to affect him later in life."

He gave her a tight smile; "wait here and I'll get someone to take you across to the camp." He slid out of his saddle and helped her down.

"I'll be alright by myself."

Kittal looked up at her from the ground, "no, I want someone with you just in case some of Titan's men are still around." He looked at her sternly.

"If you put it that way, thank you." She smiled at him with a hint of relief. She glanced over at the house with wide eyes.

She had never seen so many injured in one place. Spotting someone he shouted, "Da'ud!"

He re-appeared from behind a dragon, "sir?"

"Please take the Nejusana to the camp and guard her with your life."

"Yes sir."

With Lulizen safely on her way to the Suwars' camp, Kittal began checking the injuries of everyone who had been brought off the lawn alive. Some that had died were put back on the lawn. He really wanted to find Ciara's body but he had to resist the urge for the time being; deal with the living first and then the dead. As he felt the house shift, he glanced upwards and saw a small white Dragon pulling out the corpse from its place. Kittal smiled as he recognised the dragon from Smythman's estate. The dragon remarked as he put the body down on the lawn, *"there appears to have been more fighting here then on Jukirla."*

"One I should have been here for."

"You were not to know. We are all grateful for freeing us." Glancing up she added, *"someone is calling for you."*

Kittal turned and saw Rolande standing on the veranda steps.

Kittal crossed the body strewn lawn to Rolande and asked, "what is it?"

"Canaan has come round."

"Take me to him."

"This way." Rolande said as he turned and led Kittal round the house to the far side where on the shady side of the veranda was a row of injured. Canaan lay at the far end of the row, lying on his side since it hurt to lie on his wounded back.

Seeing Kittal Canaan struggled upright until Kittal, crouching down by his side, stopped him from doing so, saying at the same time with a smile, "don't want you to do any more damage to yourself, do we?"

"Tania, I saw her in the fighting and leaving with Titan. I wanted to rescue her but couldn't."

"Alright, take it easy. Was she going willingly?" Kittal asked with a shake in his voice and body, trying to control himself.

"No sir, she was tied up, could see the rope. I'm sacred of losing her. Don't let her die."

"I won't Canaan my friend, I won't." Kittal sighed deeply, having recovered from the shock a little. He stared out from the veranda.

"You are going to go find her aren't you?" Canaan asked with wide eyes of fear.

"Tomorrow. Today is nearly at an end."

"She may be dead by tomorrow!" Canaan exclaimed. He grabbed hold of Kittal by his top, something even he was shocked about, "she's my wife! My love! I don't want to lose her."

Kittal calmly took Canaan's hand off his tunic, looking down at it as he said, "I know you love her dearly Canaan, and so do I; but there is nothing that can be done today with so little of it left. Enough talking now, you need to rest. I'll bring you some poppy to ease the pain." He gave the man his hand back with a soft smile, as Canaan seemed to faint after his exertion of desperation.

Looking around the ruins of his house there were so many in need of attention and care, and not enough help to give it to everyone at the same time. He sighed; he was also running out of medicinal herbs and plants. He had already used up much of his poppy supply to ease everyone's pain. He wandered out and stared at the sunset. Looking back he saw many of the windows lit with oil lamps as well as braziers so the women could continue supporting him in caring for the injured.

He knew that before he was called back in he should take the chance to find Ciara's body before the scavengers that were gathering in the shadows found it. He stepped down on to the lawn and slowly began to wander through examining the faces of the corpses in the dimming light.

Rolande paused on the veranda and saw Kittal out on the lawn. He went back into the house and then returned outside with an oil lamp. He ran down the steps of the house and weaved his way through to Kittal, "you may want this Nejus."

Kittal turned at the voice and stared at Rolande for a moment as he tried to remember who it was. Finally he blankly said, "thank you Rolande, you'd best get back to the house."

"Yes sir, I hope you find her."

"I hope so as well Rolande." Kittal gave the young Suwar a tight smile as he took the lamp from him and turned away to continue looking. Rolande stared at Kittal's back for a moment, truly hoping that the Nejus would find his sister.

Kittal had no idea what time it was when he found Ciara, having turned the body over. He had nearly given up on finding her and found himself falling to his knees. He pulled her bloody body towards him and cradled her head in his lap as the tears rolled down his face. At that moment in time he felt completely alone in the world though he had his wife, son and daughter. He let out a sob and pressed his forehead against Ciara's cold one.

Brushing the tears away he picked Ciara's body up and headed towards the camp with her by the moonlight. He remained long enough to lay her on her bed in her tent before returning back to his house. He returned via Kite and Lupe's nest.

Hearing footsteps both dragons became alert, fearing that it may be one of Titan's men. Their eyes glowed faintly in the dark as they stared out. Seeing that it was Kittal both relaxed. Lupe asked, *"Nejus? What are you here for?"*

"I need you now Lupe as you are dominant male." Kittal replied to the dragon's question.

"Are you sure you want me now?"

Kittal nodded as he reached out to place a hand on the dragon's neck.

Lupe was planning to object though he shouldn't but at the touch of the Nejus he knew he could not object. He allowed Kittal to climb on his back and then he rose into the air. Kite and Ozi watched them rise into the night sky. Kite knew what was about to happen and was glad that she wasn't leader. She drew Ozi closer to her and settled down to try and sleep though she was more likely to wait for her mate to return.

In the house, all that were still awake looked up as they heard a dragon roar loud and clear in the night air. The villagers went to the windows and doors to watch as Lupe let out a stream of fire across the dead of the battle, burning them all. As he finished one trip across the lawn he roared again, letting all know of the dead. Kittal stared straight ahead, out into the night sky, trying not to think of the island men whose families would never know of what had happened to their child or partner. He joined Lupe in the last roar, though his was one of anguish.

Once Lupe had returned to his nest and Kittal had walked back to his house He leant on the veranda's balustrade looking out over the garden. He watched the small flames dancing in the darkness and the embers glowing red as the fire ate its way through the bodies. His face was empty of emotion, having withdrawn into himself. He watched to make sure that it didn't spread and engulf the whole valley as in places it was threatening to, villagers silently watching with him with shovels and buckets of water on the lawn below.

The faint light of dawn was beginning to appear over the horizon when he slipped into the tent where Lulizen was sleeping for the moment. The fire on the lawn had died down, and most of it was now glowing embers. He sat on the low bed and then fell sideways and rolled on to his back. He rubbed tired eyes. Though he hadn't wanted to wake up Lulizen he had and she asked, "tired?"
He turned and looked at her, surprised to hear her voice, "exhausted."

"You've been working hard, come closer and I'll hold you."
Lulizen replied softly. She held out a hand. He rolled on to
his side to face her. She shuffled closer and took him into her
arms and kissed the top of his head. Ozanus stirred where he
slept in a bundle of blankets but didn't wake up. Lulizen
didn't move as Kittal fell asleep.

Twenty-Five

He was sure he had heard Tania, so much so that he started awake as he heard himself calling out, "I'm coming Tania!"

He stared and saw Lulizen looking at him from the tent's entrance. Behind her he could see that it was bright outside. Fearing the worse he asked, "what time is it?"

"Late."

"No!" He exclaimed. He had promised Canaan and himself he would go find and rescue Tania with the new day. He rolled off the bed and headed out. Lulizen moved aside and asked with fear, "where are you going?"

He paused and looked at her, "I am going to get Tania." Knowing she wouldn't be able to dissuade him she replied to his departing back, "be careful."

Kittal didn't reply as he went to find Kite and get her saddled.

They found themselves following a trail of wounded and dead; of man and dragon as some of the Suwars had chased after the invaders and then lost their lives. He knew he should stop and check for any living but he had to rescue Tania. He had promised to always protect her and he couldn't if she was being held by his vengeful brother.

Flying over Linyee he saw it had once again been burnt. Half of it smoked still but the town was recovering and had no need of his help. They waved up to get his attention but he ignored them. He had more important things on his mind then the need to be a caring ruler. For once his family came first. He pushed Kite on.

As they flew along Kite feared that Kittal was not ready to take on his brother. She feared he wasn't in the right frame of mind or had the strength needed. Also he hadn't had time to plan or even have a proper night's sleep. She didn't say anything on it as she didn't want him to get angry with her. Cautiously she asked, *"what do you plan to do?"* That seemed to wake him up. He drooped in his saddle and with a sigh replied, *"I don't know Kite."*
"Should we turn back?"
"No." Kittal said harshly, *"Tania has been with Titan long enough, he could have done anything to her. I should have been there to protect her and I'm going to make up for it now."*

They circled the castle with Kittal trying to see whether he could spot either his brother or daughter anywhere though the windows. Softly he ordered Kite to roar. She did willingly. At a window Titan appeared and smiled, glad to see that his older brother had finally arrived. He shouted, "glad to see that you have arrived! Took your time didn't you!"
"Where is she Titan?! You know your problem is with me and not with her!" Kittal replied aloud as he guided Kite closer to the window, "let her go!"
Titan reached to one side and dragged Tania into view. She looked across at her father through wide eyes, "father!"
"Let her go!" Kittal exclaimed.
"No! There appears to be some things which need to be explained and you are going to tell her."
"What have you been telling her?!" Kittal demanded with fear, "don't play with her mind Titan, it's not fair on her."
"It hasn't been fair on me either, you haven't told her the truth."
Kittal searched his mind trying to work out what truths there were that needed to be told.

All he could think of was Abbitha's death. He gulped in fear as he wondered what Titan was going to trick Tania into believing.

Though he didn't want to land he knew he needed to for Tania's sake. As he slipped out of the saddle on to the battlements he said to Kite, *"keep your distance, I don't want you to frighten Titan. Come when I whistle."*

"Yes sir." She flew off to a short distance and hung in the air to watch the proceedings.

It wasn't long before Titan appeared with Tania. She broke free from his hold and ran up the steps and along the battlements to Kittal. He gave her a tight hug and murmured, "I'm sorry I wasn't there to stop this from happening."

"He keeps telling me that you have been lying to me all my life. I'm sure that's wrong but…"
Kittal placed a finger to her lips, "sssh, don't worry. I'll get this over with and then we can go home."

"The battle? Canaan?"

"Canaan is well. He hasn't been badly injured." Kittal smiled.

"That's a relief." She returned the hug as Kittal had cut through her bonds as they had been talking.

Titan arrived at the top of the steps and Tania became only a distraction. Stiffly Titan said, "Kittal."

"Titan." Kittal clutched tight to his dragon-handled knife. Tania was horrified to see her uncle produce a knife of his own from his robes.

Spotting it Kittal pushed Tania out of the way as he saw Titan adjust the knife to throw. She was about to protest but then Titan threw the knife. She turned as a knife clattered to the battlement, Kittal's knife. Kittal clutched his stomach. Getting his daughter out of the way meant this eye wasn't on his brother. Titan's knife handle now stuck out between his fingers. Tania's eyes shifted to looking at her uncle and she exclaimed, "why?!"

"Otherwise he won't speak the truth." Titan replied emotionlessly.

She turned back to her father as he dropped to his knees with a moan. He pulled the knife out causing more blood to soak into his clothes. To him she said, "I'll get you out of here. Where is Kite?"

"Not yet." Kittal moaned. He looked up at Titan, "so what lies have I told?"

"Abbitha."

"My mother killed herself because of you raping her." Tania said turning to look at Titan and then down at Kittal hoping her father was going to support her in what she had just said. Kittal turned his head away from her in embarrassment. She shook in her fear and asked nervously of her father, "it's not true?"

He shook his head reluctantly. Titan smiled with pleasure as he saw the relationship between father and daughter begin to crumble. Ruthlessly he gave Tania the truth, "I never raped her, she was my love. Your father killed her for that."

"She loved us both." Kittal corrected, looking up at his younger brother.

"Ha! What a pack of lies she gave to you. She loved only me."

"But she didn't join with you. You were barely a man."

"She was barely a woman." Titan retorted.

"She was old enough to understand what was expected of her and she failed in that. She should have known better."

"She only wanted you for the power and title. I was her love." Titan couldn't help smirking. He went on, "she joined with you out of pity. You would never have found anyone otherwise. She was with me more often than you and that is why Tania is my daughter! I have waited too long for this moment. I should have claimed her sooner, while you were absent but," he shrugged. He hadn't really been that interested until Kittal had come back and tried to dominate him again.

"Stop it." Tania protested. She looked from brother to brother, not at all sure who to believe.

She was confused. One of them was her father but which since both appeared to have been sexually active with her dead mother. She couldn't understand how a woman could love a pair of brothers and then let their love for her turn into hatred for each other. She wondered whether her mother had been playing then against each other to see which would make the better mate. At that thought she couldn't believe that she may have had a mother like that and didn't want to even think that she would ever become like that.

She was brought out of her confused thoughts by her father who was trying to explain to her what had happened, "she had to die. She disgraced herself with her adultery and it was tainting me as well. She could not be allowed to affect my name. Doing it with my brother in my bed with you sleeping next door was the last straw." He kept his eyes fixed on her as he finished. An image of his grandfather clapping over the fact he had killed his young wife with his bare hands flashed before him and he grimaced at the thought.

He let out a long low moan of pain at the thought he was causing his daughter so much hurt as well as the physical pain he was in. Tania crouched down and pressed a hand over his, "keep it pressed against it father to slow the bleeding."

"I never thought he would use you to try and wrest the title from me." He said softly and then looked at Titan and said sternly, "you are getting neither."

Tania said to her father, "don't talk."

"You shouldn't be comforting him Tania." Titan said angrily as he saw he hadn't managed to ruin the father-daughter relationship. He saw Tania look up in confusion and smiled slightly. She asked, "why?"

"I am your father, not him."

"Is that true?" She turned to look at Kittal, hoping for a truthful answer. She caught his eye and held it. Not standing the look he turned away. Seeing Abbitha's eyes looking at him he couldn't help it. He wasn't going to admit that he didn't know who Tania's real father was, embarrassed at the fact he didn't. In his heart he knew she was his, but that look had made him feel confused within himself.

Tania lent back from where she crouched by his side and stared at Kittal and then stood. She looked at the two brothers beginning to panic, who was her father? She stepped backwards, not realising how close to the edge she was. Seeing how close she was Titan began to shout a warning but then she slipped off the edge and found herself falling backwards. She stared upwards, her mouth wide in a scream, calling for the man she had always known to be her father, "KITTAL!"

She saw a hand appear but it was too late to stop her fall.

He lay on his side, blood dripping on to the wall, his body straining as if he held her tight. He cringed as he heard Tania hit the courtyard. He opened his eyes and openly glared at Titan, "that was your fault, there was no need to confuse her like that. She is my daughter through and through, and you know that."

"Are you sure?" Titan sneered, seemingly forgotten that Tania had fallen to her possible death on the courtyard's surface, "didn't you hear what I said? I was bedding Abbitha more that you were."

"That is in the past, but this is the present and I'm not going to let you live for another moment if I can help it." Kittal replied emotionlessly, making even Titan feel nervous, "She. Is. My. Daughter." Every word was defined as he spoke sternly at his brother. He slowly and unsteadily got to his feet with his knife in his hand.

Titan knew he had to kill his older brother before he managed to carry out his threat. He went for his brother, determined to wrest Kittal's knife from his hand and kill him. They struggled against each other.

Kittal found the last of his strength to grapple with Titan and push him against the crenelated edge of the wall, taking him by surprise. He pulled Titan up and held him tight against his chest, his arms trapped and his knife at his brother's throat. Into his ear he hissed, "this is it Titan. This is my land and I am the ruler not you, and Tania is my daughter!"

He pulled the sharp blade of the knife across Titan's throat. Blood spurted out and Titan slumped in Kittal's arm. He let the body fall on to the stonework and his knife clattered on it as he sagged against the battlements. He shook as he stared blankly into the distance, a blood covered hand covering his mouth.

He barely moved when Kite landed on the castle's walls, her claws chipping the stonework. Cautiously she asked, *"is it over?"*

"It's over." He forced himself to stop shaking as he slowly turned to look up into her grey scaled face. He forced himself to the steps down into the courtyard and to Tania's still body.

There was no movement from her as Kittal touched her, feeling her gently all over to work out where she was injured. Blood seeped from between her legs. The fall had been too much and the foetus had died and her unconscious body had expelled the dead child. Kittal bowed his head. He wondered how he would tell Tania when she woke. Kite landed in the courtyard and softly said, *"I'm sorry I couldn't catch her, I couldn't move."*

"You weren't to know it would happen." Kittal replied as he felt over Tania. Kite didn't want to ask but knew she had to, feeling guilty for not trying to catch Tania, *"is she.....?"*

"The Gods have blessed her. She is just alive, but that is all I can say for the time being. We need to get her back and hope and pray." He climbed on to Kite with her help. Carefully, as if Tania was her own daughter, the Dragon lifted Tania up so that Kittal could get her on the Dragon's back and hold her there. He added, *"we'll take Titan back with us as well, for burial. He deserves it though he was our enemy. It is best not to harbour bad feelings for the dead."*

"As you wish Nejus." Kite rose into the sky and turned so she could pick up Titan's body with a back claw

Twenty-Six

Arno limped over to where Rolande stood watching the last glow of the lawn pyre. Rolande glanced round, "what do you want?"

"You know the man with the scar on his face?"

"I do."

"Who is he?"

"He is Kittal, Nejus of Keytel, high chieftain of the Suwars and Lord Defender of all dragons."

Arno whistled, impressed by the titles. He never thought that the man he had followed in the woods would be so important.

Before he could ask more Kite landed on the ash covered lawn. Rolande ran across to help his lord from his dragon. Arno watched as Kittal carried the body of a woman through the house with pain etched across his face. He made to follow but was pushed out of the way by Canaan who was as white as a sheet. He wanted to protest but the look on Canaan's face silenced him. Rolande appeared at his side looking pale and he asked of the man, "what's wrong with her? Who is she?"

Rolande glanced at the boy, "that is the Nejus' daughter."

Inside Tania's bedroom Kittal lay her on her and Canaan's bed. He glanced up briefly and saw Canaan enter. In a frightened whisper Canaan asked, "what happened?"

"Get me my medical books, and my bag of plants. You should be resting but I need you. Get me the twisted candles as well, the incensed ones. Rolande, get some Suwars and head towards Linyee and check on how they are doing. It was attacked again as Titan's men retreated."

"Yes Nejus." Canaan and Rolande said and then left the room to obey. On his own with his daughter again Kittal brushed the hair off her face. He promised her, "I'll get you better if it's the last thing I ever do, you are that important me."

With the candles slowly burning around her and the room in darkness apart from the small flames Kittal began an incarnation. Canaan hung in the background, watching and hoping. He had noticed Kittal occasionally grimace and almost faint away once and felt concerned for his Lord as well. Nervously he asked, "what is wrong with her?" Kittal turned and looked at his servant and son-in-law, "she is paralysed from the neck down. She fell from the battlements of the castle."

"How?"

Kittal turned back and began the next part of what he was doing; mixing a poultice which he would then rub along Tania's spine to reduce the swelling and bruising.

It was late when Canaan drifted to sleep. Kittal wished he could join him especially as he knew he needed the rest for his stomach wound to heal. He couldn't though and wouldn't let himself do so. He had promised Tania that he would get her well and that was what he was going to do. He knew he could heal dragons but he had never tried a human. He had wanted to many times when examining some of the wounded but hadn't dared to since he had no idea what would happen if he did. He was ready to sacrifice his life for Tania's if that was the way it had to be. He now had Ozanus as his heir so his life wasn't as important anymore, especially with Titan dead as well.

He glanced over at the sleeping Canaan as he took a deep breath. With hands that had a slight shake he placed them on Tania's spine; one at either end of it. He knew she had broken bones but the fact she would have to rely on others was something he didn't want her to have to do. He closed his eyes tight, concentrating only on Tania's broken spine, blocking out the pain from his stomach wound. He didn't really know what to expect but he began to lose the feeling of his legs. It moved up his body, through his arms and chest. As he fell backwards from lack of control of his own body he was sure Tania no longer had a broken back.

The shaking of the floor woke Canaan. He stared around and then saw Kittal shaking on the floor with a stomach wound, which was obvious in the candlelight. He crawled across, "Nejus? What's wrong?"

"Get me to my room Canaan." Kittal turned his head to look at his servant through wide scared eyes.

"What about Tania?"

"She is unconscious, she'll sleep it out and her bones will heal."

"And her back?"

"Healed. I took it to save her from a life of misery."

"Wait here, I'll get some help." Canaan scrambled to his feet and hurried from the room to find help. He returned quickly with Rolande. Rolande exclaimed, "Nejus, you are wounded, why didn't you say?"

"There was something more important to do." To Canaan he said, "once I'm in bed get Lulizen."

"Yes sir."

Kittal fainted away with pain that finally he could no longer ignore.

Arno saw Kittal carried to his own room. He had sat half-awake most of the night, too curious to go to sleep. He didn't dare enter Canaan's bedroom but seeing that something had happened to the man he looked up to he followed them. In the doorway he asked, "what's wrong with him?"

"This is private." Canaan snapped.

"Ssh Canaan. We are all worried but there is no need to take it out on the lad." Rolande said,

"He aided in this. If they hadn't gone with Titan then he would never have attacked and then Tania wouldn't have been taken and our lord would never have had to save her and put his own life at risk." Canaan pointed out bitterly and turned his back on Arno. He was scared and taking it out on the boy and knew it. He was hiding the fact he felt powerless to look after his master and his wife. Tania would know what to do but she was in no fit state to help.

"Can I help?" Arno whispered.

"No."

"Just go Arno." Rolande reluctantly.

Arno stepped out of the way as several women from the village arrived to clean Kittal and stitch up his stomach wound.

Tania woke to the low murmur of voices which were coming through her ajar bedroom door. She wiped sleep from her eyes as she tried to work out where she was. She remembered being at her uncle's castle and being on the walls of the castle with her father and uncle arguing with each other. She remembered that Titan was suggesting that her father had killed her mother and that she was really his daughter and not Kittal's. And then falling. She thought of her unborn child and put her hand to her stomach and found that it was no longer swollen. A sob escaped as she had been looking forward to being a mother.

Realising that there was someone hovering close by she turned, vaguely hoping to see her father, Kittal, and definitely not Titan. She had questions for him.

She was relieved to see that it was Canaan as it meant she didn't have to confront her father just yet. She saw his face alternatively moving from worry and joy. She registered the worry first and sat up, "father?!"

"He healed you but you will still be weak. Our child, it is gone." Tears began to fall down his face. With all the stresses of the last few days telling his wife that they had lost their child was the last straw.

She looked down at her right arm and saw the bandage and couldn't think how it had been injured. Glancing round the floor of the room she saw her father's books, candles and plants scattered about. She realised that she must have been seriously hurt for her father to attempt to heal her himself with his gifted. She said, trying to stay calm, "take me to him Canaan." She held her arms out, forgetting that she had seen him fall injured in the battle.

Canaan picked her up, finding strength from somewhere deep within him. He carried her through the house to Kittal's bedroom. As they passed by the wounded each gave the other an equal amount of staring. They knew who she was though she didn't know them. All were looking solemn, as they knew what Kittal had done for the love of his daughter. He had earnt their respect and their gratitude for they could have been left on the lawn to be burnt to death.

Canaan placed her on Kittal's bed. She sat on the edge of it and took hold of her father's hand. She looked at everyone present and all they saw were her tears of fear. Though Lulizen was red eyed herself a new instinct told her that Tania needed her and she held her tight. Softly she lied, "he'll surprise us all by recovering."

"He did it for me and the last thing I was thinking about was that I hated him for not telling me the truth. I know Titan was lying about me being his daughter, I feel it in my heart. At that moment in time I didn't though. He has shown me so much love and I don't think I could ever repay it all."

"Just be the daughter you have always been."

Tania began to shake as she sobbed into Lulizen's chest, "I'm unworthy of being his daughter, of being a wife. I have lost his grandchild."

"No you aren't. You are a good wife and daughter. Its only your worry and fear coming out." Lulizen replied, sternly at first and then more calmly as she held Tania tight, "he needs your love more than ever at the moment so don't think you are unworthy. He's proud of you and there was nothing you could do about the child. There is plenty of time to create another." She lifted Tania's head and smiled calmly at her. Tania gave her a small smile back and then looked at Kittal, holding tight to his hand. He stirred and everyone in the room froze but his eyes remained closed. His breathing remained shallow as he fought the pain and fever that had come.

Softly Lulizen said, "go wash and dress as I need you by my side." She didn't want to push Tania away but she needed her in a fit shape, ready to support her as much as she would support her friend and daughter by marriage.

"What for?" Tania frowned.

"There are people from every town of Keytel, I think, come to re-affirm their loyalty to your father and I don't think I can do it on my own."

Tania nodded in understanding and gave Lulizen's hand a squeeze, "we'll do it together."

Before long they stood on the veranda together in their red robes, each giving the other strength. Lulizen held her son in her arms. Standing either side of them were Suwars eyeing up the delegates warily. All of them had come from towns who had shown themselves disloyal to their Nejus by siding with Titan.

Tania gave a nod to the Suwar who stood closest to her. In a booming voice he ordered, "bow before your Nejusana and future Nejus."

The delegates lowered themselves to the ash covered ground and lay there waiting for their punishment. A silence filled with the smell of fear and death descended on the group. The two young women glanced at each other. They had already discussed what they would do. There had been two options, punishment or mercy. If they had felt any rage it had long since left them. They didn't want any more pointless deaths. Lulizen gulped before speaking with a slight shake in her voice, she had no training for this, "I have decided there has been enough deaths. Be grateful I have shown you mercy for if my husband stood here now he might not have been so lenient."

A sigh of relief ran through the kneeling delegates.

Lulizen held up a hand and silence returned, "but… if I hear that you do not honour us then I'll be the one to bring about your punishment." She turned and stalked inside before they saw her shaking with fear. She sank to the floor and let Canaan take her son as Tania came in, "you did well."

"We did well." Lulizen tensely smiled, "now let us hope he lives for I don't think I could rule till our son is old enough."

"They won't be doing anything foolish for a while I think." Da'ud remarked as he came in, "they've gone now, all looking sheepish."

"I should think so too. We should have executed them all." Rolande added with anger, "if it wasn't for them..." He stopped talking when Canaan glared at him and he realised his Nejusana was gulping back tears. Sheepishly himself now he muttered, "I'll make sure they all leave."

"Now we have some funerals to arrange." Canaan remarked. He didn't want to bring it up but the bodies of brother and sister were beginning become bloated in the heat.

"Let us sort it all out." Da'ud suggested, "and let the women get back to our lord."

"Thank you Da'ud." Lulizen sniffed and gave the Suwar a grateful smile.

Word reached the dragons of what Kittal had done for his daughter. They all gathered on the lawn in the ashes after the delegates had left. Behind them the rising moon glowed red in the twilight sky. Lupe and Kite stood slightly forward from the rest with Delia beside her daughter. To her daughter Delia repeated, *"the Nejus needs to be taken to the temple."* She'd already tried telling her several times and had been ignored.

Kite looked at her mother, *"what are you talking about mother? He isn't fit to be moved."* She saw something in Delia's eye and added, exclaiming, *"no, you can't."*

"I can. He has an heir to teach and that can't be done from a bed or chair. Anyway I am old. Life has run its course for me daughter. It is time I joined Narl in the sky. I couldn't help his father so let me help the son instead."

Kite didn't try to object; she understood what her mother was saying. She knew she would willingly give her life up for the Nejus but she had a daughter of her own to teach. She said softly, *"Canaan needs to be told then."*

Delia nodded her aged head. She moved away from the group to spread her aged wings and then flew off to her old nest.

Canaan stepped on to the veranda to give the dragons an update of Kittal's condition but he didn't get a chance to say much as Kite said, *"The Nejus needs to be taken to the temple before the new dawn and the moon descends. Don't protest, don't ask why."*

"I... I..." Canaan stumbled over his words. He wanted to ask but seeing the dragon's look he changed his mind. He felt sure he didn't really want to know out of fear that whatever the dragons were going to do may kill or harm Kittal more. He headed back in and told the others what Kite had said. The women looked afraid, not understanding what Kite had meant by the instruction she had given Canaan. Tania asked her husband, "why?"

He shrugged his shoulders with a face empty of expression. Solemnly he remarked, "we should just obey, they know more than us."

Kittal was laid in the centre of the ruined temple, the cloth banners in the arches flapped in the wind. He stirred but didn't wake. Canaan dapped at his Lord's feverish forehead. As the dragons began to gather all the people present stood back out of the way instinctively. They felt that this was something that few human eyes had ever seen and felt honoured to even be there. Lulizen held Ozanus and Tania lent on a crutch next to Canaan. Rolande stood with Leanne and their week old son. Arno had quietly followed the family, staying far enough back so they wouldn't ask him to leave.

The dragons gathered close together, encircling Kittal and Delia. There was a low murmur of their voices, which slowly rose in volume. Delia stood on her old hind legs and let out a roar at the moon which seemed to shine brighter even with the hint of dawn showing on the horizon. All the dragons stopped singing and joined her in her roaring, all looking up at the sky.

With all the noise Kittal stirred and opened his eyes. He stared wide-eyed up at Delia's bleeding chest where she had pulled scales from it. He knew that even if he hadn't been paralysed, he still wouldn't have been able to move. He had an idea of what was going to happen and felt fear creep into his heart. He had read of this dragon ritual but had never thought to see it, let alone be the one to receive it. Another roar from Delia rang clear in his head forcing him to close his eyes.

Delia dropped on to the claws on her wings and pressed her vulnerable breast against Kittal and spread her wings to receive the joint rays of moon and sun, each of which held magic that only the dragons knew about. Kittal could feel the dragon's heart beating in unison with his and cautiously opened his eyes to find the dragon's neck just above his head. He opened his mouth as he felt his heart stop with the dragon's.. He saw Delia fading in front of his eyes and wondered whether it was truly happening. His heart started again and his mouth formed the word, *"Delia?"* As if he hadn't even been paralysed he reached up only to find himself touching air. He looked around at all the other dragons with his eyes wide. He felt feeling come back to his legs and with a hand cautiously touched his stomach. He could feel nothing there, as if he had never even been wounded. Nervously he asked to any dragon who would answer him, *"what happened?"*

"Delia has joined her mate in the sky. She sacrificed herself for you." The Jukirlan dragon explained.

"How?"

"That we are not allowed to tell you."

"I..... I understand, I think." Kittal replied. He tried to stand but Kite stepped closer, holding a wing over him to stop him from standing. To him she said, *"though you may have been*

removed of a broken back and stomach wound you are still weak from loss of blood. You will still be weak. Stay down, don't try to move."

Outside the circle of dragons everyone was looking at Canaan, wanting him to translate what they could just about hear. Though he was straining his ears Canaan couldn't catch enough which would be worth translating. He murmured to Tania, "I can't Tania, I can't hear enough. I don't think I would even if I could. This is something between them and the Nejus which doesn't involve us."

"I understand." Tania replied. She looked up at Canaan and he put an arm around her.

The dragons began to part, all looking solemn as they did. Canaan ran to Kittal who still lay on the stone floor of the temple. With wide eyes Kittal looked at his servant, still feeling in complete awe of what had happened. He didn't know whether he could speak now that the moment had gone. He could still sense Delia within him. He turned his head as Canaan crouched by him. He mumbled to his servant, "I've been healed, Delia….."

"Can you stand sir?"

"Not yet."

"You look dazed sir."

"I know." Kittal said vacantly, "who is here?"

"Your family."

"Ciara?"

Canaan looked worried at that, thinking that Kittal had lost some of his memories. Nervously he answered, "she is dead Nejus. Titan is also dead, you killed him sir."

"I did?" Kittal sounded surprised. After a moment he said to Canaan, "get me home Canaan."

"Yes sir."

His body craved rest but his mind was aware that there were two funerals to be organised. When he was told that everything was under control he was grateful that

Canaan and Da'ud were dealing with it all. All he would have to do was attend.

With the sun at its highest Kittal, dressed in his robes, slowly approached the grave, leaning on his servant a little. Tania and Lulizen with Ozanus followed behind.

Brother and sister lay together in a wide pit. Ciara lay dressed in her dragon armour surrounded by some of her personal items, weapons and saddle. Beside her Titan had been dressed in a plain tunic and trousers. The Suwars and dragons stood back as the group approached.

Kittal took a deep breath and stepped away from Canaan and approached Ciara's dragon. They bowed to each other as Kittal solemnly asked, "do you wish to follow your rider?"

The dragon had already been thinking about this as she nodded, "I do. I have no mate or child."

Kittal nodded in understanding.

He drew out his knife and held it as a dagger and pressed it deep into the Dragon's breast, and into her heart. The Dragon showed no pain as she pulled herself away from the knife and then slumped to the ground. It was agonising watching her die, her blood pooling on the ground but finally she gasped for one last breath and her large eyes closed. In a flicker of an eye the large body vanished. He placed his knife back in its sheath to be cleaned later and turned back to the graves. Kittal knelt by the edge of the grave. He saluted to her, pressing his fist against his chest.

Tania passed him a few flowers. Kittal tore the petals off them and threw them over his siblings' graves. They floated down white, red and blue. Brushing tears away Tania helped her father to his feet and together they stepped back.

The gathered dragons roared out in their mourning while all the people present remained silent. In the house the Suwars and villagers, injured and uninjured, closed their eyes to reflect for a moment.

Back outside Kittal let out a cry of anguish and dropped to his knees as the soil was being thrown back into

Titan and Ciara's graves. He couldn't believe his siblings were now both dead. Lulizen stepped forward and gently placed a hand on Kittal's shoulder to try and comfort him. He turned and looked up at her and she saw the sorrow in his eyes. Softly she said, "you are not alone. You have me and Ozanus as well as Tania and Canaan."

"I should have been the first to die if everything had been right in this world, but now I will be the last."

Kittal drew in a deep breath and stood making Lulizen step back. He didn't acknowledge anyone as he headed back to the house. There would be time later to mourn his family as there was the all-night vigil ahead.

They sat as two separate groups. Leanne sat with her brothers and sisters around one fire recounting tales of their mother. Kittal sat in front of his own. He silently recalled a time when the three of them had all been close and wished it had remained so.

In the morning the injured Jukirlans that were fit enough to be up gathered on the lawn and began clearing the ash from it and transferring it to a pit they had already dug for it and any charred bones. Kittal appeared from the bushes and they froze. They didn't know what he would do to them now.

He barely glanced at them as he crossed the lawn to his home where Chief Tomas was supervising the mending of the roof. The Chief paused in his order as Kittal walked up on to the veranda. They embraced as Kittal said, "how many did you lose?"

"About half of the men but we will survive. This is our home and we were honoured to help defend it. What are you going to do with all of them?" He gestured with his head.

"They are going to have to go soon." Kittal answered stiffly as he turned to look at them working, "but I do not think they will be welcome back on Jukirla either."

"Did you manage to free the dragons there?"

"Yes and Jukirla is now mine." He rested his hands on the veranda's railings, "but this is not the end as I need to reinstate my authority over all of Keytel."

"Your wife and daughter have already started it."

Kittal raised an eyebrow, "I was not aware of this."

"It was while you were unconscious. By all accounts they did a good job." The Chief remarked with a rueful smile.

"It seems I need to speak to my wife."

"I think she has earnt the respect of the Suwars now and not just because she has given us your heir."

"Thank you Tomas." Kittal smiled with pride before walking into his house.

He acknowledged Arno's hesitate presence and beckoned the young man into his study. Arno waited for the Nejus to sit before cautiously asking, "sir?"

"Arno?" Kittal responded as he reached for a pile of correspondence he needed to look through. There was no time to rest for a ruler of a huge country and Senspanta needed to be reminded who ruled them.

"I don't want to go back to Jukirla."

"What do you want then?" Kittal looked up.

Arno approached Kittal's desk, "I want to stay here and learn more."

Kittal paused and looked at the boy with the very beginnings of a beard. He gave the boy a nod, "your training starts today. Go and find Canaan. I will get a message to your parents."

Arno grinned and ran from the room. Kittal smiled briefly before returning to his work until Lulizen appeared with Ozanus.

About the Author:

I am an independent author, writing since my teens. I don't have the money or the weight of a publishing house behind me so every sale and every review is truly appreciated.

Please follow me on Instagram @f_garstang_author for more about me and the books I have self published or am working on.

Fanny Garstang

Printed in Great Britain
by Amazon

86386107R00129